Praise for *Sophie's World*

'A marvellously rich book. Its success boils down to something quite simple – Gaarder's gift for communicating ideas' *Guardian*

'An *Alice in Wonderland* for the 90s . . . *Sophie's World* is being talked up as philosophy's answer to Stephen Hawking's *A Brief History of Time* . . . this is a simply wonderful, irresistible book' *Daily Telegraph*

'An extraordinary achievement' *Sunday Times*

'Challenging, informative and packed with easily grasped, and imitable, ways of thinking about difficult ideas' *Independent on Sunday*

'A terrifically entertaining and imaginative story wrapped round its tough, thought-provoking philosophical heart' *Daily Mail*

'A unique popular classic' *The Times*

'Seductive and original . . . *Sophie's World* is, as it dares to congratulate itself, "a strange and wonderful book"' *TLS*

Jostein Gaarder was born in Oslo in 1952. *Sophie's World*, the first of his books to be published in English, has been translated into 60 languages and has sold over 40 million copies. He is the author of many other bestselling, beloved novels and children's books, including *The Orange Girl*, *The Christmas Mystery* and *The Ringmaster's Daughter*. He lives in Oslo with his family.

Also by Jostein Gaarder

Sophie's World
The Solitaire Mystery
The Christmas Mystery
Hello? Is Anybody There?
Vita Brevis
Through a Glass Darkly
Maya
The Ringmaster's Daughter
The Orange Girl
The Castle in the Pyrenees

The World According to Anna

JOSTEIN GAARDER

translated from the Norwegian by Don Bartlett

WEIDENFELD & NICOLSON

First published in Great Britain in 2015
by Weidenfeld & Nicolson

This paperback edition published in 2016
by Weidenfeld & Nicolson
an imprint of the Orion Publishing Group Ltd
Carmelite House, 50 Victoria Embankment
London EC4Y 0DZ

An Hachette UK Company

1 3 5 7 9 10 8 6 4 2

Copyright © 2013 H. Aschehoug & Co. (W. Nygaard), Oslo
English translation © Don Bartlett 2015

The rights of Jostein Gaarder and Don Bartlett to be
identified respectively as the author and translator of this
work have been asserted in accordance with the
Copyright, Designs and Patents Act 1988.

The publication of this translation has been made possible through
funding from NORLA, Norwegian Literature Abroad.

A CIP catalogue record for this book is
available from the British Library.

978 1 780 22918 8 (Mass Market Paperback)
978 0 297 60975 9 (eBook)
978 1 409 16053 3 (Audio)

Typeset by Input Data Services Ltd, Bridgwater, Somerset

Printed in Great Britain by Clays Ltd, St Ives plc

www.orionbooks.co.uk

Contents

Sleigh Ride

O n New Year's Eve, for as long as Anna could remember, the families in her village had gone up to the mountain pastures on a sleigh. The horses had been groomed and dressed, and the sleighs had been adorned with bells and flaming torches to cut through the darkness. Sometimes a piste-basher was sent up in advance so that the horses wouldn't get stuck in loose snow. But every New Year's Eve without fail they went to the mountains, not on skis or scooters but on horse-drawn sleighs. Christmas was a magical experience, but it was this sleigh ride into the mountain meadows that was the real winter adventure.

New Year's Eve was a special time. Normal rules did not apply, and everyone mixed freely. On that evening they left one year behind and entered the next. They stepped over an invisible boundary between what had been and what would be. *Happy New Year! And thank you for the old one!*

Anna loved this time of year. She couldn't decide which part she liked the most: the ride up the mountain to celebrate the last hours of the old year, or the trip back down, wrapped up tight in a blanket with Mum's, Dad's or a neighbour's warm arm around her shoulders.

But on New Year's Eve the year Anna turned ten, no snow had fallen either on the mountain plateau or on the lowlands. Jack Frost had long held the countryside in his icy grip but, apart from the odd small drift, the mountains were untouched by snow. Even the high mountain terrain lay bare beneath the open sky, stripped of its winter cloak.

Adults muttered about 'global warming' and 'climate change', and Anna made a note of these new terms. For the first time in her life she had a sense that the world was in disarray.

But to the mountains they had to go, whatever the conditions, even though the only possible way to get there would be by *tractor*. They would also have to go during the day – without snow on the plateau, it would be too dark to see your hand in front of your face at night. Even torches would be of little use, and tying them to the tractors and trailers would look silly.

So it was that five tractors and trailers wound their way slowly through the birch trees carrying delicious food and drink. Snow or no snow, they had to raise a glass to the New Year and perhaps organise some games on the frozen meadows.

The absence of snow had not been the only talking point that Christmas. Over the holidays, reindeer had been spotted down by the farms, and people joked that Father Christmas might have left behind a couple on his rooftop travels.

Anna had sensed that there was something scary, something alarming about this. Reindeer had never strayed down to the villages before. Anna had seen pictures in the newspaper of farmers trying to feed a poor, frightened creature: *Wild Reindeer in Mountain Villages* the caption had read.

The procession of tractors set off, and Anna was in the first trailer with a few of the other children. The higher they climbed, the more the frozen landscape looked like glass. It must have rained before the frosts came, trapping water underneath.

They caught sight of an animal carcass on the roadside, and all the tractors stopped. It was a reindeer, frozen stiff, and one of the men explained that it had starved to death.

Anna didn't quite understand. But later, when they were up in the mountains, she saw that the whole area was frozen over. Every last pebble and plant was trapped below the sheet of ice.

They passed Lake Brea. Here the five tractors stopped again and the drivers switched off their engines. They were told the ice was safe, and everyone rushed out on to the lake, adults and children alike. The ice was transparent, and shouts of excitement rang out as they realised they could see trout swimming beneath their feet.

Out came balls, hockey sticks and toboggans. But Anna walked on her own along the shore, studying the frozen heath. Under a thin membrane of ice she saw moss and lichen, crowberries and black bearberries with crimson leaves. It was as though she had moved into a more precious, a more refined, world. Soon, though, she spotted a dead mouse . . . and another. Under a dwarf birch she found a dead lemming. By now Anna understood, and she no longer felt as though she was on an adventure. She had known that mice and lemmings survived winter in the mountains by hiding between bushes and scrub, under soft blankets of snow. But if there were no blankets of snow, the mice and lemmings would not survive.

Now Anna was in no doubt why the reindeer had strayed down to the lowlands. And it had nothing to do with Father Christmas.

Six Years Later

Dr Benjamin

Anna was sitting at home with her parents in their old timber house. It had been dark for hours, and her dad had lit candles on the mantelpiece and windowsill. It was 10 December, and there were only two nights left before she turned sixteen.

Her mum and dad were huddled on the sofa. They were watching a film about the Pacific Ocean, an adventure story about naval battles. Or was it a documentary about one of those legendary eighteenth-century sea captains? Anna wasn't sure; she wasn't really following.

She sat at the dining-room table casting the odd glance at the Pacific as it flickered across the television screen. She was holding a large pair of scissors and was cutting articles out of old newspapers.

In August, Anna had started upper secondary and, after just a few days at the new school, she got to know Jonas, who was in the class above her. They quickly became good friends and for a few days they pretended to be a couple, as a sort of game, but then they realised that was exactly what they were.

Anna sat hunched over her cuttings with a big mug of tea. She smiled at how suddenly life could change.

But she had been prepared for changes – after all, she was turning sixteen. Today, at last, she had been given her Aunt Sunniva's old ring. She had known for a long time that she would inherit it on her birthday. But she had been given it today because her mum was going to a conference early the next morning. They had a formal dinner – her mum had been to the bakery and brought back a marzipan cake with a red rose on top – and after the meal, the ruby was unpacked from an old jewellery box and presented to Anna. She wore it for the rest of the evening and, while she was cutting up the newspapers, she could not keep her eyes off the ring.

It was more than a hundred years old – some

said several hundred years. And there were so many exciting stories about the jewel.

She had also been given the smartphone she had asked for. She could now get online with just one touch of the screen – but that was nothing compared to how wonderful her ring was.

But the ring wasn't the strangest thing that had happened to Anna that year. The strangest had to be her trip to Oslo in October.

Ever since she was small, Anna had been told she had a lively imagination. If she was asked what she was thinking, she would reel off endless stories, and no one had thought this was anything other than a good thing. But that spring, Anna had begun to believe some of the stories. She had a feeling that they were being sent to her, perhaps from another time, or even another reality.

In the end, Anna's parents persuaded her to have a chat with a psychologist. After several sessions, the psychologist said she would like Anna to be examined by a psychiatrist in Oslo. Anna didn't mind this. She had nothing to be ashamed of, she thought; in fact it made her feel special.

But she had set one condition: that her parents couldn't come. Jonas offered to go with her. Her mum and dad insisted that one of them had to accompany her. They reached a compromise: she was allowed to take Jonas, but Mum would go too, if she promised to sit in another train carriage.

So the three of them turned up at the *Rikshospital* where Anna had her appointment with the psychiatrist. But neither her mum nor Jonas was allowed to go in with her, at least not at first, and Anna could see that this was a terrible blow to her mother. She had wanted so much to be involved. But for now she had to sit and wait with Jonas.

Anna liked Dr Benjamin from the moment she saw him. He was in his fifties and had long, greying hair tied into a ponytail. In one ear he had a tiny violet star, and in the breast pocket of his black jacket he had a red felt pen. There was a playful glint in his eyes and he watched her intently.

She could still remember the first thing he said after they had shaken hands and he had closed the door behind him. He told her that Lady Luck was smiling on them because his next appointment had been cancelled. They had all the time in the world.

Sunlight poured into the white room and Anna

looked out at the red and yellow leaves on the trees. She spotted a squirrel scurrying up and down a pine tree.

'*Sciurus vulgaris*,' she said. 'Or the common squirrel. But in England it's not that common any more. The American grey squirrel has killed them off.'

The psychiatrist's eyes widened and Anna wondered whether he was impressed by what she had said. As he swung round on his chair to see the squirrel, Anna noticed a photograph in a red frame on his desk. It was of a beautiful woman – was she his daughter or his wife? Anna wanted to ask him, but the next moment he turned back and obscured the picture, and she forgot.

She had of course wondered what a psychiatric examination might be like. It wasn't easy to imagine how a psychiatrist would look inside her head, but she had assumed he would begin by studying her eyes with a special instrument; the eyes were the window to the soul, after all. She had supposed that he would also try to peer into her head through her ears, nose or mouth – psychiatrists had trained as doctors, unlike psychologists. She wasn't sure how much she'd actually believed that the doctor would do these things, but they had spooled through her mind like reels of film. She had definitely been frightened that he might hypnotise her and empty her mind of all its secrets. Anna didn't like to lose control and she didn't want to reveal *all* her secrets.

But all they had done was talk. The psychiatrist asked her a lot of interesting questions, and the conversation was so much fun that Anna dared to ask him questions back. What about the doctor? Did he ever come up with strange stories? Did he also have dreams where he was a different person? Had his dreams ever come true?

Eventually, Dr Benjamin reached his conclusion.

'Anna,' he said, 'there's nothing to suggest you are ill. You have an unusually active imagination and an uncanny ability to visualise things you haven't experienced. This may feel overwhelming sometimes, but there is nothing wrong with you.'

Anna didn't think there was anything wrong with her either. She had been convinced she wasn't ill. She felt duty-bound to remind him that she sometimes believed her own fantasies. She said it felt as though the things she thought and imagined came to her from the outside, and not from within.

He sat there nodding.

'I think I got that,' he said. 'You may have such an active imagination that it seems to overflow. You can't believe that you made it all up yourself. But imagination is a quality everyone possesses, to a greater or lesser extent. Everyone has their own dream world. Not everyone, however, can remember what they dreamed the night before. This is where you appear to have a rare gift. You take what you dream at night . . .'

Anna laid all her cards on the table:

'But I still get a feeling that the dreams come to me from another world. Or from another time.'

The psychiatrist nodded again. 'The ability to hold beliefs lies deep in our natures. We, as humans, have always felt as though we're in contact with supernatural forces, whether gods, angels or ancestors. Some people have claimed that they've seen these figures with their own eyes, or even met them. Some people are more willing to believe than others. Everyone is different. Some people are almost unbeatable at chess or mental arithmetic. Others are almost unbeatable in the field of imagination or belief, and perhaps Anna Nyrud is a world champion!'

Anna looked out at the sunlight playing on the vibrant autumn leaves.

'Had you believed that all the bees in your garden were controlled by the CIA, and they were buzzing round your house to spy on you, then maybe you might have a serious mental disorder—'

'How do you know I have a garden?'

'The psychologist's report said you told her you'd prefer not to meet a reindeer in your garden.'

Anna laughed. 'She didn't have a clue what I was talking about. But I love the garden. And the bees . . .'

'Oh yes?'

'Bees are part of nature, like you and me. Obviously they aren't controlled by the CIA. They're controlled by their genes. I also think they're a kind of indicator of how healthy the planet is.'

'Exactly. And what you're saying to me isn't crazy or what we psychiatrists call a "bizarre notion".'

While they were talking he occasionally glanced at the computer screen. He was doing it again now, and Anna realised the document claiming his attention must have been a report from the psychologist in her village.

'Is there anything you're afraid of, Anna?'

She answered at once. 'Global warming.'

The psychiatrist gave a start. He was clearly an

experienced doctor but he had been surprised by her answer.

'I beg your pardon?'

'I mean, I'm afraid of climate change. I'm afraid that we're risking our climate and environment without a second thought for future generations.'

The psychiatrist paused for a few seconds. 'And that is a valid fear – which unfortunately I cannot help you with. If you'd said you were afraid of spiders it would have been different. In cases like that we talk about phobias, and then we treat the patient; we expose them to the thing they're scared of. But we can't treat your fear of global warming.'

She looked Dr Benjamin in the eye and then glanced at the earring in the shape of a star.

'Do you know how many billions of tonnes of carbon dioxide we've released into the atmosphere over the last ten years?'

To Anna's surprise, the psychiatrist didn't miss a beat. 'I think today there's about forty per cent more carbon dioxide in the atmosphere than there was before we seriously started burning oil, coal and gas, cutting down forests and farming intensively. It's more than 600,000 years since the CO2 level was so high, and the problem is man-made.'

She was impressed. Not many people had these answers at their fingertips. 'There is already so much gas out there,' she said, 'that no one can predict the consequences. And the emissions are getting worse . . .'

Dr Benjamin was leaning forwards with his palms on the desk. He looked down for a second or two then he peered up at her again. He seemed almost dumbfounded.

'Well, this isn't my line of work. But let me tell you that I share your concerns about the burning of carbon. Although, come to think of it, perhaps this *does* have something to do with psychiatry . . .'

While he paused she said, 'Go on. I'm listening.'

'Sometimes I ask myself whether we live in a culture that intentionally *represses* fundamental truths. Do you understand what I mean by that?'

'I think so. We try to forget unpleasant things.'

'That's exactly what I meant.'

Anna had a brainwave. She had no idea why the thought had popped into her head; it was as though it came from another world. She heard herself say, 'What would you have said if I told you I was afraid of Arabs?'

He chuckled. 'I would have suggested you spent some time with Arabs. I think that would be the most effective treatment.'

'Cool . . .'

'But we don't treat patients' concerns about global warming. I suppose the question is: wouldn't we be better off looking for a way to treat *lack* of concern. Obviously we shouldn't allow ourselves to grow accustomed to this threat. We must try to come to terms with it.'

The psychiatrist had spoken to her like an adult from the beginning, and she liked that very much indeed. He had spoken to her as an equal. Even so, when he asked if she belonged to an environmental organisation, she was taken aback. She had not expected to be asked that in a doctor's surgery. But she was the one who had brought the subject up.

She said there were no environmental organisations where she lived. Everything revolved around going to school and going to work, tinkering with cars and motorbikes and then partying and drinking at the weekend.

'The young man you came with, is he your brother?'

She laughed.

'Oh, no, that's Jonas. He's just my boyfriend.'

She thought she sounded cool when she put it like that. *He's just my boyfriend.*

He laughed along with her.

'Is Jonas as interested in the environment as you are?'

She said: 'He's in the year above me and takes physics, chemistry and biology. So he's learning a bit about the world, of course.'

'Of course.'

'And global warming isn't just a matter of opinion any more. Either you know about it or you don't.'

'I agree with you, Anna. It wouldn't surprise me if less than one per cent of the Norwegian population can explain what the carbon balance is.'

Anna felt her heart leap a little. The carbon balance was something she had been discussing with Jonas recently. 'Can you? I mean, can you explain what the carbon balance is?'

After switching off the computer and clearing away the papers on his desk, the psychiatrist turned to Anna. He began by explaining the carbon cycle. Plants absorb carbon dioxide from the air by photosynthesis and the carbon attaches itself to living organisms. Carbon dioxide is released into the air when animals breathe and when organic material breaks down. The carbon balance is the remarkable equilibrium which exists between the amount of CO_2 released into the atmosphere by volcanic eruptions and the amount which is broken down by the wind and weather, and becomes part of the earth's crust. This balance had been constant for many hundreds of thousands of years, and humans had had no effect on this cycle. So they were able to ignore it.

He went on: 'All the carbon stored in fossil fuels – oil, coal and gas – has been "parked" and withdrawn from the cycle for millions of years. But this delicate balance . . .'

Anna plucked the words from his mouth: ' . . .this delicate balance has been upset by burning oil, coal and gas, which pumps carbon dioxide into the atmosphere.'

'That's what I was just about to say. Even though the amount of CO_2 released by human activity is only a small fraction of the amount in the natural cycle, the excess cannot be locked up in the earth's crust. So there's more and more CO_2 in the atmosphere.'

'And it accumulates,' Anna said.

'Precisely. You know all this as well as I do. If you eat more calories than your body needs every day, you will begin to put on weight. It's the same with CO_2 in the atmosphere.'

'And then the earth gets warmer. The more CO_2 there is in the earth's atmosphere, the warmer it gets. Then the ice melts and the glaciers too, and that makes matters worse because snow and ice reflect sunlight, but sea and mountains don't. So the earth gets even warmer . . .'

'You're quite right. That's what we call amplified feedback.'

'. . . which can cause the tundra to melt. Methane and CO_2 are released into the atmosphere. Methane is also a powerful greenhouse gas, and the earth just continues to heat up. There's more and more steam in the atmosphere, and it gets warmer and warmer. Now it's Greenland's turn to melt, and next it may be the Antarctic . . .'

Dr Benjamin held up his palm, and Anna realised he was trying to stop her. But she wasn't going to let this chance to share her knowledge go. 'The greenhouse effect could get out of control and, worst-case scenario, the world's temperature could increase by six to eight degrees. By then all the ice on the planet may have melted and the sea may have risen by tens of metres . . . In Norse mythology they had a word for what could happen on Earth. They called it Ragnarok.'

Dr Benjamin had got up to say goodbye and see Anna out. But before he opened the door, he said, 'Perhaps you and Jonas should set up a pressure group in your village. That would be the best course of action. As a psychiatrist I know it's not healthy to become consumed by your worries. So, if I may give you a piece of advice it would be: go for it. Make something happen.'

He rummaged through his pocket and passed Anna his business card.

'Just ring or email me if there's anything you'd like to talk about. I live on my own now – you're welcome to get in touch.'

When they emerged into the waiting room, the psychiatrist shook hands with Anna's mother and Jonas. He looked them both in the eye and said: 'Thank you very much for lending me Anna. She's an inspiration – you're lucky to have her around every day.'

Her mother was so confused that she curtseyed.

On the tram down to Oslo she asked why the psychiatrist had a star in his ear – as though Anna would have had any idea. But her mother and Jonas didn't know what she and Dr Benjamin had talked about so Anna made it up: 'He's got a star in his ear because he's realised we're living on a vulnerable planet orbiting a star in space. Not everyone realises that, and only those who do can walk around with a violet star in their ear.'

Both Jonas and her mother were gaping at her.

'Obviously a grown man wouldn't walk around with a star in his ear unless he knew he was living on a planet orbiting a star.'

Anna's mother took the afternoon train, but Anna and Jonas stayed, walking hand in hand through the Oslo streets. They went to Frogner Park and Aker Brygge, then they visited the Ecology Centre in Grensen, where many of Norway's environmental pressure groups were based. On the train home that night, they made plans for their own group. Jonas had agreed to form one with her.

He would be in charge of recruitment. Anna had suggested this because Jonas was the most popular boy at school, and he could sign up the girls without even trying. He laughed: 'But I didn't realise it was a girls' group.'

'No, of course not. But if you sign up the pretty girls, the cool boys will follow.'

Anna's job would be to supply the information. That was why she was sitting at the table now, two days before her birthday, snipping away. There had been a lot in the news recently about climate change – a conference in Qatar had failed.

Anna put down the scissors and sat in front of the TV with her parents. The film showed Captain Cook observing the transit of Venus above the idyllic island of Tahiti. Venus was moving in front of the sun – this was such a rare phenomenon that a hundred years could pass before it happened again. In Captain Cook's time it was important to observe this transit in several locations – only then would it be possible for astronomers to calculate how big the solar system really was.

There was something romantic about a British captain travelling to an exotic Pacific island to calculate the distance between the earth and a planet named after the goddess of love. But according to the film, the captain and his crew were more preoccupied by the women on the island, and by romance of a more earthly nature.

The music faded and the credits rolled, and then the evening news started: the Nobel Peace Prize had been awarded to the EU. Twenty-one heads of state had been in Oslo. And a Norwegian aid worker had been taken hostage in the borderland between Kenya and Somalia. Her name was Ester Antonsen and she worked for the World Food Programme.

Anna said goodnight to her parents and went to her room. Tonight she wouldn't have to set an alarm because tomorrow there was no school. But she had promised to call Jonas as soon as she woke up.

It had been a special day. She had inherited Aunt Sunniva's ring and been given a phone which half the school would envy. She had cut out all the climate articles she could find. And the day after tomorrow she would be sixteen!

Anna was excited by what she might dream. She knew she would plunge into another reality the minute she fell asleep.

The Terminal

She opens her eyes and her name is Nova. Everything feels different and new.

She wriggles up the bed and is overwhelmed by light. As she reaches to grasp the source, it shines more brightly. The terminal screen above her says Saturday 12 December, 2082.

She can see the contours of the room where she has been asleep. The walls are as red as blood. Rain pelts down on the narrow window which stretches from the wooden floor to the slanted ceiling.

The terminal beeps and a picture appears on the screen. It is a small monkey with eyes like saucers. Another primate is declared extinct. It had disappeared from the wild a long time ago: the South American cotton-top tamarin's eco-system had burned up and dried out. The very last member of the species has died in captivity. It is sad. It is tragic.

The machine beeps again. Another iguana, also from South America. Extinct.

She can feel her cheeks burning. But there is nothing she can do – once again the machine comes to life, and pictures of an antelope are beamed to her. It has been declared extinct, this very second, by the International Union for the Conservation of Nature (IUCN). For a generation, no living soul has seen a herd of antelopes, gnu or giraffes in what used to be called the African savannah. Now the herbivores are gone, the beasts of prey have gone too. Some of the species have survived in zoos, but now they are dying out too.

She installed the Lost Species app a long time ago. Of course, she could uninstall it at the press of a button. But she considers it her duty to notice the earth's species and habitats dying out. She is angry. She is furious. But there is nothing she can do . . .

The most significant cause of this mass extinction is global warming. It got out of hand decades ago. Only a hundred years earlier, this planet was outstandingly beautiful. In the course of this century it has lost its charm. The world will never be as it was. It has been many years since people stopped pumping out CO_2, but climate gases, once released, cannot be taken back. The planet has passed several tipping points. Humans are no longer driving global warming. It is the Earth which is doing that now.

She touches the screen and enters EarthCam. She can use the terminal as a remote control, and projects the image on to the roof above her head. She pulls herself up and surveys her planet.

What's the weather like at the North Pole? She looks up at the Arctic Ocean, dazzling and blue. The whole room is filled with light. There is no ice in sight, and today there is almost no wind. Only the ripples on the sea show that this is a live shot. She can see the little buoy on which the camera is perched. It is some decades since the last polar bear was seen in the wild, although there are still a few, in zoos.

What does the Pacific Ocean look like, the Indian Ocean? Many of the old coral islands are already under water; whole countries have been washed away. Only buoys show where the land used to be. Some have floating signs: the Maldives, Kiribati, Tuvalu. In the crystal-clear water Anna sees ivory-coloured buildings a metre below the surface:

old temples, mosques and mission churches. Sunken civilisations, exotic paradises from times gone by.

And what of the Siberian tundra? It's bubbling and boiling. She chooses sites she has visited before, staring at the gossamer-thin projection and imagining methane gas coming from the swamp. It is going to get even warmer, they say.

She touches the screen and calls up the latest satellite pictures. The globe rotates slowly. Aren't the continents smaller than they were only a few years ago? Haven't more coastal towns been swamped? The ice caps over Greenland and the Antarctic are definitely smaller than they were last year.

But what is it like where she lives? She finds footage from the Hardanger Plateau. It is late in the year and there are still some leaves on the birch trees. Seagulls and crows flutter above treetops. She zooms on to the heath and forest floor. A field mouse peeps up between tree trunks and a red fox appears, sinking its claws into the mouse.

Some of nature remains, but only the crumbs from the rich man's table. What she sees is wonderful, but she will not be fobbed off by it. She has the right to live in nature which is intact. Not holey, like a Swiss cheese.

She decides that for the rest of the day she wants to see only pictures and films from the beginning of her century. It takes just seconds to apply the filter. She inputs 12 December 2012 as the cut-off date. From now on she can only download websites which went live before this date. For the rest of the day she can revel in images of the earth before 12.12.2012. Parts of the world were wonderful back then. She switches off the IUCN app. She can put it back on the next morning, and then it can beep to its heart's content – because she will not accept letting even a mollusc or violet be declared extinct without her knowledge. It is no coincidence that she chooses 12.12.2012 as the cut-off date. She knows it was around about then that the eco-systems began to really break down. And that date is her great-grand-mother's sixteenth birthday.

She searches the archive and begins by watching the anthropoid apes. As soon as she sees the video of dwarf chimpanzees she gets butterflies in her stom-ach. They are so funny to look at she has to laugh. They were animals – yet so like humans! They had their own personalities. The young apes in the bushes play just like human children. Imagine! That only a few years ago these funny creatures roamed

Earth! Then she turns to gorillas. The animals she is watching form the bridge between humans and the rest of nature. The gorillas look miserable and perhaps that is because, on some level, they know they are on the way out. Now they have gone for good, never to return. She watches a couple of clips about red orang-utans. They are from Borneo and Sumatra. A mother orang-utan is feeding her baby. It looks like a healthy, lively baby, but it could be the last orang-utan born in the wild . . .

When Nova's great-grandmother was young, she could have watched exactly the same clips; they had been made in her time, and had ended up in the archive. But Nana had spoken to people who had actually been on safari in Africa and seen living apes *in the wild*. That won't happen again. Humans will never see a living chimpanzee or gorilla that isn't in a zoo. Anna's generation was the last that ever would.

She watches clips. She is reassured by the fact she has thousands of excellent ones to choose from. She picks a BBC film presented by David Attenborough. Nova sits wide-eyed, staring at beautiful pictures of a bygone world.

She watches living things swarm around a coral

reef. She sees molluscs, crawfish, seagrass, turtles and fish in every colour of the rainbow. It is as though God had hand-painted every single one of them. But Nova is painfully aware that everything she is watching on the screen above her bed has gone for ever. Now there are no coral reefs and no shoals of brightly coloured fish. The sea is too acidic – for more than a hundred years it was forced to swallow millions and millions of tonnes of CO_2. It was as though a demon had been released and had decided, *Right, that's it. That's enough! All these beautiful species must suffocate!*

She looks up at the screen again and finds herself in what was once the great Amazon rainforest, now the world's largest savannah. She watches an old film about butterflies. Their magnificent patterns give her goose bumps, but she knows all too well that most varieties now only exist in electronic form.

Never before could so many creatures be seen on camera. Never before could so few creatures be seen on Earth.

She reads what people wrote in newspapers and online at the beginning of her century. It's all still there: the words, the pictures and the music. One article reads: 'We cannot pass on a world which is poorer than the one we inherited . . .' Ugh! She clicks on another: 'I can imagine the misery of our grandchildren and great-grandchildren, deprived of resources, of gas and oil, and also of biodiversity . . .'

She shakes her head. There was no shortage of warnings.

She wonders whether Nana had written anything when she was young. If she finds anything now, with the search filter on, it would have been written before Nana turned sixteen. She searches for Anna Nyrud. She tries several search engines and eventually a result appears. It is a letter – to Nova!

Dear Nova. The hairs on Nova's arms stand on end. *I don't know what the world will be like when you read this, but* you *know* . . .

How is that possible? The letter is dated 11 December, 2012 – the day before Nana turned sixteen. But how was it possible for Nana to write a letter to Nova more than fifty years before she was born?

Nova checks her search dates. They're still exactly the same as they were before. The terminal is receiving nothing written after 12.12.2012.

How could Nana have known that she would have a great-grandchild called Nova? Was she psychic?

Is she still psychic?

Nova gets up from her bed and walks across the room. She turns off the screen and then plays an audio file, another artefact from the turn of the century.

A man's voice says: '. . . from the end of the eighteenth century, fossil fuels have tempted us like the genie in Aladdin's lamp. "Release me," the carbon whispered. And we gave in to temptation. Now we're trying to force the genie back into the lamp.'

Raindrops beat against the window. Nova sits under the slanting ceiling and tries to see through the rain. A long time ago there was a petrol station in the valley – concrete and rusting iron still mark the spot. Now, hardly any cars pass through, but caravans of Arabs on camels still roam the land. North Africa and the Middle East are no longer habitable, and their refugees are migrating north, settling on the north-western coast of Norway.

She crouches down and presses her face against the glass. Now she can see better. Below, in the rain, a small huddle of people stands next to three weighed-down camels. Smoke is coming from a fire . . .

Blue Light

Anna was woken from her dream by sirens. She squinted through sleepy eyes and saw blue lights flash through her room. But she didn't want to be woken up – she *mustn't* be woken up. Her dream was important and she had to go back and sort something out . . .

This wasn't the first time she had been woken up by a siren. A few weeks earlier, Jonas had stayed over in the cushion room – so-called because the sofa was heaped with cushions. Old Aunt Sunniva had embroidered them with scenes from fairy tales. When Anna was very small, her parents would tell her the stories, and later she would imagine herself as the tiny embroidered figures, acting out their tales and living their lives.

But when Jonas had slept over, the household was woken in the middle of the night by howling sirens. The vehicles hadn't just sped by; they had stopped in the road below. Anna and Jonas hadn't needed to wake each other up. They had almost collided on the landing. Seconds later, Anna's mum and dad had charged down the stairs after them.

More vehicles arrived from both sides of the valley: police cars, ambulances and fire engines. In the bright blue flashes of light, they glimpsed the outline of a tanker that had overturned on the slippery road. They were stopped from getting any closer by the police, who had started cordoning the area off. Later they heard that there had been a terrible risk of explosion and fire because the overturned tanker had been carrying thousands of litres of petrol. When the police officer screamed at them: 'Go back! Turn round, for Christ's sake!' the fire crew had already been laying a foam blanket.

Anna, Jonas and her parents turned around and shuffled back. At first they stood in the garden watching the drama unfold, then Anna sat in the kitchen with Jonas and listened to the radio while her mum made hot chocolate and her dad sat in front of the fire smoking his pipe . . .

But this time, Anna didn't allow herself to be fully woken by the sirens. She was in another world, and she was on a mission.

Great-Grandmother

There is a knock at the door, then a figure appears to drift into the room. Nova turns around and sees it is Nana. She is wearing a blue kimono.

Nova sits down on the edge of her bed and looks up at the old lady. She recognises her, of course, but she also senses something mysterious, something foreign. Nana's face is small and wrinkled. It is Nana's birthday. Today she is eighty-six years old.

But something is different about her, distorted. A shiver passes through Nova. It looks as though every breath could be Nana's last.

She is wearing the ruby ring. Nova knows that there is a connection between this ring and the sense that Nana's time is running out. Nana arrives in the room like a messenger from another time. She places two lined fingers on the red jewel. Then she says:

'You're thinking about the ruby, aren't you, Nova?'

Nova nods. It is as though Nana can read Nova's mind.

The old lady fetches a wooden chair from the desk and sits down in front of her.

'Today I'm going to tell you about the birds that lived in the mountains back in my day. I can still hear the plaintive whistle of the golden plover.'

Nova squirms. Does she really want to hear this? Can she be bothered to listen to the ancient woman any more?

'You don't need to tell me anything,' Nova says. She is filled with bitterness. 'All I want to know is how to get the birds *back*.'

She glances up at Nana. The old lady has a look of deep sorrow on her face. Or remorse. Perhaps it is remorse.

But Nova shows her no mercy.

'I want monkeys, lions and tigers, too. I want them all back. Why can't you understand? I want bears and wolves in Norway. And that funny sea parrot – what's it called? The puffin! And the curlew

– don't forget about the curlew! I want bearberries and alpine speedwell and glacier buttercups and dwarf willow. Did you know that the dwarf willow was a bush even though it didn't grow more than five centimetres high? Or was it you who told me that?'

The old lady's shoulders twitched.

'But Nova . . .'

'Do you know what I want? Shall I tell you? I want a million plants and animals to come back from extinction. No more, no less, Nana. I want to drink clean water straight from the tap. I want to go fishing in the river. And I want this clammy winter weather to end.'

'Nova, please. Nova!'

'I'm just saying I want the world that you had at my age. And do you know why? Because you owe me that!'

'Nova, stop it!'

'Or would you rather I sent you off into the forest? Give me back my world. Give me flocks of reindeer on Hardanger Plateau, in Jotunheimen and in Rondane. If you can't do as I say, you might as well leave now.'

'But Nova . . .'

'Do you know what else I wish? I wish everything on this planet could be given a second chance. Just imagine if that wasn't asking too much. It could be like in those shooting contests. If you miss the first time, you get to go again. I just think you should give me back the world. Wouldn't that be a turn-up for the books? If people didn't cry over spilled milk. If they stopped wallowing and made amends instead. Just be a nice, sweet Nana and give me back all the animals and plants. Then we can talk about birdsong.'

For a very short moment she glances at Nana's eyes. They are quivering. They are frightened and sad. But Nova continues: 'What am I babbling on about? I'm talking rubbish! It's impossible to change anything. We can't go back. Isn't that right, Nana? Or are you going to tell me there's a genie of the lamp that can help us?'

Nana struggles to sit upright in the chair. She looks afraid, as though her great-grandchild might strike her at any moment. With a clenched fist. Hard.

But the old lady says: 'Yes, my dear Nova. That's the sort of thing I would have said.'

'What?'

The old lady caresses the mysterious ruby. She

looks dreamily at her great-grandchild:

'Perhaps the world *can* have another chance . . .'

Little old Nana. What is she burbling on about now? But she says it in such an enticing way that Nova is carried along.

'What do you mean?' she whispers. 'A miracle?'

There is a glint in Nana's eye. She nods firmly then smiles.

They are friends now. Nana was sixteen once, too. Who hasn't been?

But what can they do? She looks at the blood-red walls and up to Nana in her blue kimono: 'Perhaps we can shout back through time and tell the people who lived before us to show a bit of consideration? We just have to make sure we shout loudly enough for them to hear.'

The old lady shakes her head: 'That's impossible. But I think I know another way.'

'Go on. Is it something supernatural?'

'I don't know, my child. Perhaps it's the most natural thing in the world.'

A smile spreads across Nova's face. 'I think I understand,' she says. 'You're going to try to make contact with the people who lived on Earth before us, so you can warn them. You're going to show them what the future will look like if they don't stop exploiting nature. Come on, Nana. Is that what you're going to do?'

The old lady nods mysteriously.

But then Nova thinks about this more. She pivots off the bed and peers through the narrow floor-to-ceiling window down on to the road. The camels are still there with a small cluster of people.

'It's impossible.' She sighs. 'Nature is so damaged – we've passed the point of no return.'

'Are you absolutely sure?' Nana's smile is bewitching. Again she is playing with the ruby.

'Is it something to do with the ruby?' Nova asks sweet, kind Nana. 'Will that stone give us back our reindeer?'

Nana nods again, and her great-grandchild laughs.

'That's what I thought,' Nova says. 'I've always known there was something magical about that old gem.'

Nova wonders what else she can ask for: 'Can I have the eagle owl back too? Just a couple of them, please. And otters, and chequered blue butterflies . . .'

There is no stopping Nova now. She thinks quickly, so quickly she gets dizzy. It is a wonderful moment. At any second an avalanche of wishes might be fulfilled, like when a shower of shooting stars bursts across the night sky. But who can think as quickly as stars can fall? She braces herself:

'Can I bring back a million species of plants and animals?'

'Yes, you can, my dear.'

'And their habitats too? There's no use saving the animals two by two. Plants and animals must have something to live off, they have to *thrive*, so the rainforest must be restored, the acidification of the sea must be reversed, the mountain temperature must be brought down a few degrees, and the African savannah must be watered. But you know this because you're not daft, you really aren't . . . Oh – to think this is even possible!'

Nana grasps at the red ring. Then she speaks in a solemn voice. She sounds almost like a sorcerer: 'Soon you shall have the earth back the way it was when I was your age, but you must promise me you will look after it. For this is our very last chance. From now on we should always be on our guard. *There will be no more chances.*'

There was something odd about the sound of Nana's words. It was as though they were being swallowed by a deep cellar or coughed up from a great cave.

But she wasn't finished: 'And so we shall meet again in seventy years' time. Then it will be you who is called to account.'

Nova is overwhelmed. This feels like the world's greatest conjuring trick.

The room begins to sway, and when Nana smiles she looks like a child – she looks far too childlike for a woman of her age. She leans her head back against the old chair – it is as though she has lain down to die. Then she starts singing in a gruff voice; it sounds as if she is chanting at a Witches' Sabbath.

'All you birds, be you so frail . . . come back as once before! Tern and cuckoo, thrush and quail . . . chirrup forever more! Larks rejoice up in the sky . . . trilling a new spring on high. Frost and snow, they had to hie. We have sunshine and light!'

The Red Boxes

Anna woke with a start and threw open her eyes. There was such a strange smell in the room, so strong and stuffy. She switched on the reading lamp above her bed and looked up at the walls and the light-blue slanting ceiling.

She had been dreaming . . .

What a strange dream it had been, so mysterious and optimistic.

She had been living in the future and in the same attic room as now, but in the dream the walls had been as red as blood and on the ceiling there had been a large flat screen.

She heard the titmice outside. When the weather was nice they twittered in the winter, too. But then she heard a car engine revving down at the petrol station. A car door slammed. And then there was another car, coming from the west. And then another, at speed.

She touched the ruby. It was an old treasure that had been in her family for nearly a hundred years. Her Aunt Sunniva had gone to America with her fiancé, but he had mysteriously drowned in the Mississippi a few weeks after they got engaged.

Anna's family liked to call the engagement ring 'the ancient heirloom', as though it represented something magical, a wonder that would outlive them all. Anna was now the owner of that ring. It had been passed down from Anna's grandmother, who had died the year before. Her grandma had inherited it directly from Anna's great-grandmother's childless sister, Aunt Sunniva.

There had been something in her dream about that ring . . .

She had dreamed that her name was Nova and that she had a great-grandmother called Anna, who had been born on the same day as her. Today was 11 December 2012, and tomorrow it was Anna's sixteenth birthday.

On her finger, this great-grandmother, or Nana, wore a ruby set in gold, the spitting image of the ring Anna was wearing now. And that was because it *was* the same ring – worn on the same finger! In the dream Anna had been her own grandchild, and through the eyes of that grandchild she had seen herself as a great-grandmother.

It wasn't so remarkable that Anna should dream she was her own great-grandchild. Once, she had dreamed that she was Napoleon, and another time that she was a goose. But had it all just been a dream? Anna was not so sure about that. Her dream had felt so familiar and so true – not only at the time but also now, long after she had woken up.

In Nova's world, natural habitats had been destroyed, and thousands of plants and animals had become extinct. Filled with bitterness and hatred, she had turned to her great-grandmother and demanded a world where nature was as rich and diverse as it had been when Nana had been a girl. Then a miracle had taken place, for now it *was* the beginning of the century. The feeling of being catapulted back seventy years was still fresh. Anna and the whole world had been given another chance and, in some mysterious way, this was all connected to the ring.

What a day lay ahead of her! She felt as though

she was standing on the threshold of a new era. Everything could now start from scratch. The world was new, spanking new, and pardoned. All the extinct plants and animals had been reborn. A million species had been returned to their habitats.

Those species were still in great danger. There had been no shortage of scary reports. But it wasn't too late to recover the earth's biodiversity. The world had been given another chance.

She remembered the letter that Nova had found online. In the dream it had been written by Anna to her great-granddaughter long, long before Nova was born. But what had the letter said?

She leaped out of bed, bounded the two steps across the floor and switched on her computer. She mustn't be distracted by other thoughts. She had to concentrate on remembering as much as possible of the letter Nana had written.

She typed: *I don't know what the world will be like when you read this, but* you *know. You know how the climate was destroyed, how nature was decimated and perhaps exactly which plants and animals are extinct . . .*

She couldn't remember any more. The letter had been long and she thought she might recall more of her great-grandmother's words as the day went on.

She called the document 'Letter to Nova' and saved the file.

Anna looked out of the tall, narrow window and saw that it was a sunny December day, which was great because she was off school, but she hadn't planned anything yet. The sun had just risen and was casting long shadows over the snowy landscape, but today would have to wait. She was immersed in her dream, which was still bubbling away in her brain. It felt as real as the winter's day outside. And it was hotter.

She looked down at her desk. There were a few dog-eared *State of the World* annual reports, a new edition of *The Norwegian Red List*, a journal which documented climate change, and a wonderful book called *A Gap in Nature: Discovering the World's Extinct Animals*, which her dad had recently brought home from Australia.

There were bookshelves above Anna's desk. On the bottom one Anna kept two shoeboxes that she had lined with red wrapping paper. On one box she had written *What is the world?* and on the other *What has to be done?* She kept cuttings and print-outs inside them.

In her dream, Nova had read some of the articles

from the red boxes. Anna had cut out one of them just the evening before, while Mum and Dad had been watching the film about Captain Cook.

She got up from her chair and took the boxes down from the shelf. She flicked through the papers and soon found what she was looking for:

An important basis of all ethics has been the golden rule, or the principle of mutual respect: do to others as you would have them do to you. But the golden rule can no longer only have a horizontal dimension – in other words a 'we' and 'the others'. We are beginning to realise that the principle of mutual respect also has a vertical dimension: do to the next generation as you would have had the previous one do to you.

It is that simple. You should love your neighbour as yourself. Which, naturally enough, should include the next generation. It must include absolutely everyone who will live on this earth after us.

The fact is, all of mankind does not live on Earth at the same time. All of mankind does not live at the same time. People have lived here before us, some are still living here now and some will come after us. Those who come after us are our fellow humans too. We have to treat them as we would want them to have treated us – if they had been the ones who had inhabited this planet first.

The code of behaviour is that simple. So we cannot bequeath a planet that is worth less than the one we have been allowed to live on ourselves. Fewer fish in the sea. Less drinking water. Less food. Smaller rainforests. Fewer plants on the mountains. Fewer coral reefs. Fewer glaciers and ski runs. Fewer animals . . .

Less beauty! Fewer wonders of nature! Less splendour and joy!

Phew! Anna felt exhaustion overwhelm her as she re-read the words. It was the third or fourth time she had read them, and her great-grandchild would find precisely the same words online seventy years in the future; everything that was online today would remain for eternity. All the words and images of our time floated in this information cloud.

Our poor heirs, she thought. Not only would they have to live on an ailing planet because of our selfishness, they would also have to live with the fact the warnings had been there. 'You should love your neighbour as yourself. Which, naturally enough, should include the next generation . . .' These words of caution from a distant past would be so galling to future generations – long, long after it was too late to change a single thing.

But there was more. Nova had found something else on the internet. Anna flipped through the print-outs and cuttings in the *What has to be done?* box and eventually found what she was looking for.

The root cause of both the climate problem and the threat to biodiversity is greed. But greed doesn't generally bother the greedy. Of this there are many historical examples.

If we live by the principle of mutual respect, we should only allow ourselves to use non-renewable energies if we have ensured that our heirs can cope without these resources.

It is not difficult to find answers to these ethical questions; what is lacking is our ability to put the answers into practice.

I can visualise our grandchildren's and great-grandchildren's distress – at the loss not only of resources such as oil and gas but also of biodiversity: you took everything! You didn't leave anything for us!

You took everything . . .

It was as though Anna had woken up from an intense dream, and the dream was still buzzing through her head. If only it had been a dream . . .

Her thoughts moved on to Jonas. She had promised to phone him as soon as she woke up. But he would have to wait. She had to try to remember more of her dream, and then it occurred to her: Nova had been listening to something as she moved around her room.

Anna knew the words. She had the transcript of the audio file somewhere . . . But where was it? She searched both boxes, but it wasn't there. She must have overlooked something – but what? Had there been a reason why she had forgotten to put the transcript back in its place? Slowly the reason began to dawn on her, and she took an old book down from the shelf. It was called *One Thousand and One Arabian Nights* and was in English. She had wanted to check something in this book recently, and the transcript she was looking for was there, as a bookmark.

In many ways we are living in exceptional times. On the one hand, we belong to a trail-blazing generation exploring the universe and charting the human genome, but, on the other, we are the first generation to damage the environment on our own planet in a serious way. We can see how human activity is draining resources and causing habitats to disintegrate. We are changing our surroundings to such an extent that it has become normal to talk about our era as a completely new geological age: *anthropocentric.*

Enormous quantities of carbon are stored in plants and animals, in the sea and oil, in coal and gas. This carbon is just longing to be oxidised and released into the atmosphere. On a dead planet like Venus, CO_2 makes up the majority of the atmosphere, and it would be the same here if the earth's processes didn't keep the carbon in check. But, from the end of the eighteenth century, fossil fuels have tempted us like the genie in Aladdin's lamp. 'Release me,' the carbon whispered. And we gave in to temptation. Now we're trying to force the genie back into the lamp.

If all the remaining oil, coal and gas on this planet is pumped up and poured into the atmosphere, our civilisation may not survive. Yet many see it as their God-given right to excavate and burn all the fossil fuels within their nation's boundaries. Why should nations with rainforests not do as they wish with their rainforests? What difference will it make to the global carbon balance or to biodiversity if every other country is exploiting their resources?

Anna went to the window and looked down to the busy petrol station in the valley. It was like a living fossil: it looked so old-fashioned, like a relic from another time, and yet it was still fully active.

She was reminded of something else from her dream . . .

The Umbrella

It is pelting down with rain as she walks down the steep hill underneath a red umbrella. The umbrella is big enough to shelter a whole kindergarten class. On the other side of the river there have been landslides but, above them, the main road remains intact.

She walks to the crossroads where there was a petrol station in the olden days. Now it is a kind of staging post. The Arabs tend to stop here before they set off across the mountains. The camels are given water and the refugees eat and rest. A huge bonfire is burning in the lower valley, and people are warming themselves around its flames.

She mingles with the crowd: women in long dresses and men in white tunics which reach to their feet. Her red umbrella is so wide that people have to step aside to make way for her, but some walk under the red awning and say hello. The children don't even have to duck.

The people laugh and are happy. One of the men is juggling with old oil-lamps, and the women and children are clapping their hands. Villagers are selling lamb kebabs and hot drinks. Some are selling rain gear and woollen blankets. Gold coins are exchanged.

Beyond the crowd, a boy is lying in the grass. She asks one of the women in black if he is ill. The woman looks worried and nods. 'Long journey,' she says in English.

She walks over to the boy and shelters him with her red umbrella so at least he won't get soaked by the rain. Two women follow her. Nova points up to her house and says the young man can sleep there.

The boy accompanies them up the hill, supported by the women. They meet Nana in the doorway, and Nova explains that the boy is ill. He will have to stay with them until he is well again. They put him in the cushion room. They may have to call a doctor because he looks as though he needs medicine.

The Oil

Down at the petrol station more and more cars were coming into the parking area. The drivers usually left their engines running while they went into the shop to buy hot dogs and crisps. Anna was annoyed by all the exhaust fumes the cars were pumping out as they idled there. She called them hot-dog cars. The bluish-grey fumes were sharp and clear because it was several degrees below zero, ten or more, perhaps. She didn't have an outside thermometer by the narrow window, but she had acquired a knack for judging how cold it was from the colour and consistency of the car fumes.

Anna stood in front of the window, reflecting on what she had read about oil. She had jotted down some figures on a yellow Post-it, figures she barely believed.

A barrel of oil measured 159 litres and was currently worth around a hundred dollars, or 600 Norwegian kroner. One barrel produced as much energy as 10,000 hours of manual labour. In Norway that was equivalent to six years' work. On an annual wage of 350,000 kroner that came to 2.1 million kroner. So a single barrel of oil produced energy that would have cost more than two million kroner to replace with human labour. But the average American got through twenty-five barrels of oil a year, which meant 150 years of work. This was equivalent to the average American commanding 150 'energy slaves' at any one time – to run their cars and machines, fridges and air-conditioning units, planes, factories, farms and entertainment systems . . . and that's just oil! That's before they even got to coal and gas.

Anna had often wondered whether oil might be too cheap. In the USA it was introduced around the same time as slavery was abolished. First the Texan ranches were awash with slaves from West Africa. Then they were awash with oil . . .

But only 600 kroner for six years of manual labour? That was barely a hundred kroner for a year's work. You could certainly call that a slave's wage.

How was it possible for the fuel to come so cheap? Anna had worked out her own answer to that question. Oil was so cheap because no one owned it. No one owned oil, so it had no price. All you had to do was pump it from the ground.

Oil was several million years old. It was a reservoir of many millions of years of solar energy. But because no one owned it, it could be used up just like that. A snap of the fingers and no more oil!

Anna looked down at the Post-it and shook her head.

It was probably true that oil had lifted many people out of poverty, as politicians and energy ministers pointed out. But a great many people had been lifted into a life of pointless luxury and overconsumption, the like of which had never been seen before.

Anna also held a cutting in her hand. It was an advertisement for air travel. The cheapest ticket from Moss Airport to Paris was only 119 kroner. How many cheap tickets there were, she didn't know. But the interesting part was the small print. It said, 'taxes and fees included'. 119 kroner to Paris, *taxes and fees included!* That was the same as a tram ticket in Oslo. What *wasn't* in the small print was that a return flight from Oslo to Paris had the same environmental effect as someone commuting four-teen miles a day, every day for a year. Anna had also read somewhere that a return flight Oslo–New York had the same effect as 50,000 car journeys.

Weren't we wasting resources that coming gen-erations could use? Weren't we letting batteries go flat when they should have lasted much longer? Perhaps it wouldn't be long until oil was replaced by busy hands, stiff necks and sore, aching shoulders? Wasn't Anna a witness to future generations being robbed on an epic scale?

She was still standing by the window. In her dream, farmers had been selling lamb kebabs to the refugees who were still moving through the country. Many of them were trying to make it as merchants in the north of Vestland.

Anna had to smile. What sort of dream had she concocted! But it felt as true and real as her memo-ries of going to Italy last summer. She remembered the dream better than she remembered what she'd done at school the day before.

But there was more to the dream. It felt as if it

had no end. While she had been asleep she had created a complete future universe, one which existed
in parallel with the life she was living now. If she
pulled one thread the whole thing would unravel –
episodes from the past and the future, or even from
a different now . . .

The Camels

The boy is better. He is her age, perhaps a year older, and they are sitting in the cushion room playing Ludo. She has the red tokens and he has the blue.

He says the game comes from India. The kings there used people as tokens. They played with women from their harems. Sixteen young women might stand in a courtyard, with red and white flag-stones for the squares.

The boy has managed to place three of his tokens on one square. He throws the dice again and three become four. He explains that he has won because he has a 'minaret'. They disagree on the rules and stop playing . . .

Now they are standing outside, under the copper

beech, looking down over the valley. A runaway camel is approaching the staging post. The boy turns to her and says: 'My great-great-grandfather used to travel by camel. My great-grandfather drove a Mercedes and my grandfather flew across the world in a jumbo jet. But now we're back to camels.'

He looks at her thoughtfully and adds: 'Oil was a disaster for my country. We became rich overnight, but now we're poor. How can we be rich when we can no longer live in our own country?'

The boy has to go. Another group of Arabs has gathered at the staging post. Smoke rises from their fires and steam from their pots. When Nana comes out to say goodbye, the boy takes a ring off his finger. He gives it to Nana to show his gratitude.

She is disappointed that Nana gets all the thanks. But the boy turns to her and strokes her hair. It is the first time a boy has ever stroked her hair. He says that Nana is old, and that one day Nova will inherit the ring. He says it is an Aladdin's ring and it comes from a story written down in *One Thousand and One Arabian Nights*.

She stares into a pair of dark, almost completely black eyes, and in them she senses a secret.

Archive

Anna came to, sitting on the blue pouf by the narrow window. She felt drained. She had one again just travelled seventy years back in time. The world was like a mitten, which she could turn inside out and wear both ways. She was two people. She was sixteen in 2082, and she would be sixteen tomorrow.

Her birthday was tomorrow!

She took off her ring and watched it glint in the light. This ruby was said to be the colour of dove's blood: deep red but with a tint of blue. Now Anna could see it reflected in the glass. It was called a star ruby: a six-rayed star shone from within it, and moved in the light.

She could trace the ring's history back one

hundred years. But she had heard stories about this ring which were much older. Old Aunt Sunniva had told the family that it came from Persia, although the stone itself was from Burma . . .

She sat down in front of her computer and typed in: www.arkive.org. A second later she was on her favourite website: IMAGES OF LIFE ON EARTH.

The first thing she saw was a picture of Sir David Attenborough and an Iberian lynx. Then she clicked through photographs and clips of thousands of animals and plants. She read about their habitats, as they were now and as they used to be.

Many of the planet's eco-systems had already shrunk: links with fresh, healthy zones had been severed. In Africa, plants and animals that had flourished the length and breadth of the continent were now only found in the scattered remains of primordial forest. The same was true in Europe, Asia and America. But the breakdown of biodiversity had begun much earlier in Europe than on other continents. In central Europe, beasts of prey had almost died out. In Norway more than five thousand bears were killed in the second half of the nineteenth century.

She typed *Hominidae* into the search box and

brought up six species of anthropoid ape. There were two kinds of chimpanzee, two of gorilla and two of orang-utan. Four of these were *critically endangered* and two were *endangered* according to the IUCN Red List. So all the earth's apes were either *critically endangered* or *endangered*. *Critically endangered* meant that the species *faced an extremely high risk* of extinction within a few decades, and *endangered* meant there was *a very high risk* of extinction. Only a very high risk. Well, thank you very much.

She clicked on some of the clips. They showed the same images she had seen on the slanting ceiling when she had been on the other side of the mitten. But, only a few decades on, the species shown had been extinct. The situation was not quite so hopeless now. A few members of those species still lived in the wild, in scattered oases.

As this destruction took place, man became the most populous mammal on earth. Of course there was a connection – mankind had threatened its closest relatives with extinction, not only by cutting down forests and destroying habitats but also by trapping and hunting illegally.

She searched for the world's great beasts of prey. Many were as threatened as the apes. Over the past hundred years the tiger population had decreased by ninety-three per cent. But apes and beasts of prey were not the only victims. Thousands, probably hundreds of thousands, of plants and animals were at risk because their eco-systems had been damaged or erased. And a lot of that was down to climate change.

Again she looked at the ruby. Since the ring had been made, so much of nature had simply vanished – how much more would be lost one hundred years from now?

Anna had almost forgotten the second present she had received for her birthday, but now she went to get the smartphone from her bedside table and turned it on. She had a text, her very first on that phone, and, of course, it was from Jonas:

Are you awake, Anna? Ring me?

She felt bad; she had promised to phone him as soon as she woke up, but she replied, *I'm busy, Jonas. With something important. I'll call soon.*

He replied in seconds: *OK. Take the time you need. But what could be so important on the day before your sixteenth birthday?*

Newspaper apps were pre-installed on her phone. She touched the screen and saw the front-page news:

'STILL MISSING. Ester (pictured) is still being held hostage in Somalia. Norwegian Ester Antonsen left Mogadishu International Airport yesterday morning with two other World Food Programme representatives – one an Egyptian national, the other American – and five local truck drivers. All three aid workers are now in captivity . . . The famine in the Horn of Africa has proved devastating after last year's catastrophic drought. Thousands have died of starvation, and a large number of refugees have tried to escape the region . . . The political situation has undoubtedly contributed to the suffering, but climate researchers can no longer rule out the possibility that natural disasters such as these are caused by global warming . . .'

Anna studied the photograph of the missing Norwegian. She was probably in her thirties. But hadn't Anna seen her before? Hadn't she *met* the woman? Had she been a supply teacher? Or had Anna dreamed about her?

In the past Anna had been introduced to people she had never met in real life but had seen in her dreams. She had learned it was wise not to bring that up early on. But now she was on her own, so she said the first thing which came into her head upon looking at the picture: 'Oh, how funny to meet you! I've dreamed about you!'

Caravan

She is sitting high on the hump of a camel. Four other camels are swaying in front of her. They carry blankets and other goods which the refugees will be selling at the big markets in Molde and Kristiansund. Strings of beads and sachets of spices hang from the proud animals' sides.

Nova sits in a saddle as the boy leads the camel. She is wearing a red cape, a present from one of the women. She feels like a Bedouin princess surveying the landscape from on high. The boy looks up at her and smiles.

'*Shaykhah!*'

She can join the caravan for part of the way, but she has to catch the electric bus back from Lo, further west in the valley. She has only gone along for fun, but she has got to know the boy very well, and neither of them is keen to part.

There are thirty people in the group, young and old alike. The man leading the convoy beats a drum made of camel skin while an eleven- or twelve-year-old girl dances back and forth, playing a bamboo flute.

They have crossed the bridge and started the long march towards the mountain pass. It isn't raining any more, but the land is still wet and the trees are dripping.

The river gushes through the valley, ready to burst its banks. Please let the rains stay away!

The countryside has never been warmer, wetter or greener than it is today, and the rivers have never looked browner. Norway's population has grown five-fold in forty years, not because more children have been born but because refugees have arrived in droves to the northernmost regions of the world. Scandinavia still has a lot of room for them.

She tells the boy about global warming deniers who lived at the turn of the century. They were mostly middle-aged men who said that climate change wasn't a threat and wasn't man-made.

Man-made or not, it could only be a good thing for the people of Norway . . .

'That's what I call hedging your bets,' the boy replies. 'The ostriches in Africa and the Middle East were so frightened by what they saw they hid their heads in the sand. That wasn't such a good tactic. Now they're extinct.'

Nova, sitting high on the camel, laughs. She almost has to shout for him to hear:

'Some people thought there was nothing to worry about when the Arctic ice caps began to melt . . . It wasn't as though anyone went skiing or skating up there . . . Anyway, there were large deposits of oil beneath the ice. And Norway could claim them. What was this nonsense about keeping the polar bear alive? Hadn't they done enough by saving the panda? But these men didn't realise that the melting ice was a warning that the whole planet was warming up. And now here I am on the hump . . . of a camel!'

They reach Lo. He helps her down from the camel, and soon the rest of the caravan is out of sight. The electric bus will arrive at any moment.

They stand exchanging Skype names. They promise each other that they will meet again. He shows her pictures of the tiny emirate that he comes from. But Nova cannot make anything out. All she sees is sand.

'Where are the towns?' she asks.

'The towns are still there, but they're hidden under sand.'

He flicks through the album and eventually finds a photograph of one small building, or maybe a tower, the top of which is poking up through the sand. 'That's a minaret.'

The bus comes and they high-five as she gets on board.

The Red Lists

Anna stood with her smartphone in her hand, wondering when she might have seen the missing woman. Was it when she was walking around Oslo with Jonas? They had met a lot of people at the Ecology Centre when they went to get brochures and advice on setting up a pressure group. But how likely was it that one of them would be in Africa a month later working for the UN's World Food Programme? They had spoken to someone from the Rainforest Foundation Norway, and they had chatted to a woman from something called the Nordic Development Fund. But did any of these organisations work with the UN? None of this made any sense.

She lifted up the book that her dad had given her.

It was *A Gap in Nature: Discovering the World's Extinct Animals* and was by an Australian author. The book was heavy: it must have weighed a kilo at the very least. The cover showed a dodo, a large bird from Mauritius, which was related to the pigeon and dove families, and last seen in 1681. Anna opened the book at a drawing of the last surviving species of moa bird, hunted to extinction by the Maoris at the turn of the seventeenth century. The book contained drawings of all the mammals, birds and reptiles that had been declared extinct between 1500 and 1989.

The moa and dodo had a lot in common. They were flightless birds with no natural enemies until mankind came along. From then on, they were easy prey.

Anna had read somewhere that the moa still held a place in Maori folklore. In New Zealand – or *Ao-tea-roa*, as the Maoris called it – you could still hear this lament: *No moa, no moa in old Ao-tea-roa. Can't get 'em. They've et 'em. They've gone and there ain't no moa!*

Between the book's pages, Anna found an article she had printed out off the internet.

The so-called Red Lists of threatened plants and animals come out in increasingly elegant publications with sharp colour photos of species which are *critically endangered, endangered* or *vulnerable*. As a natural extension of this trend, in a few years we will undoubtedly have some splendid coffee-table books with equally splendid colour photos of species that have already become extinct. They will be exactly the same photos as those which adorned the lists of threatened species years before, and at some point in the future we will probably talk about these species as 'photofossils', i.e. species that just managed to have themselves recorded for posterity before they vanished along with their habitats.

Isn't it ironic that the heyday of nature photography – and the advent of digital storage – coincided with mankind beginning to make serious inroads into the earth's biodiversity? But one day the dinosaurs will be passé and instead we will gaze at technicolour photographs of birds and mammals which have died out in our lifetimes.

This was sick. What right did mankind have to destroy other forms of life?

What was wrong with humanity? That was what Anna wanted to find out as soon as she could. She had an idea.

She opened her desk drawer and took out Dr Benjamin's business card. He had said she could call him. To be on the safe side, she texted him first:

What on earth is wrong with us humans? Can we talk? When's a good time? Best, Anna (Nyrud).

He replied in less than a minute. *Now's fine. I'm not at work today. Benjamin.*

'I'm not at work today.' Why had he written that? Well, if he had been at the hospital, ringing him there would have been inconvenient. But she still couldn't quite figure out why he'd mentioned that. And why wasn't he at work?

A maelstrom of thoughts began to whirl around her head. But before she could make sense of them, she dialled his number. He picked up a few seconds later:

'Benjamin.'

'Anna here.'

'Hello there. How did you know . . .?'

'You gave me your card.'

'OK.'

'Are you stressed? You sound a bit stressed.'

'Of course. Why are you calling, Anna?'

Of course? Anna had no idea what he meant by that. But she remembered why she had called him. 'Does psychiatry have anything to say about why we're destroying our own planet?'

'. . .'

'Hello?'

'You said, "What on earth is happening to us humans?" But you don't know?'

'Don't know what?'

'About my daughter.'

'Ester Antonsen!'

'Yes, that's my daughter, yes. So you did know?'

'No, no, I didn't. I've just realised this very second. And now I know exactly why I'm ringing. You had a photo of her on your desk . . .'

'Actually, it's a photo of my wife when she was Ester's age.'

'Really? They must look so similar . . .'

'Can we change the subject? I *am* a bit stressed but I still need someone to talk to.'

'The psychiatrist is off work and he needs *patients* to talk to?'

'Yes, indeed. The human mind is a complicated thing.'

'Well, what would you like to talk about?'

'Have you seen any reindeer recently?'

She laughed. 'Yes, I'm still seeing them. I think they're spying on me . . . for Father Christmas.'

'Perhaps they're trying to find out what you want for Christmas?'

'Maybe . . . I think everything will work out for Ester, and I'm not saying that because I believe in Father Christmas. You've got to think positively, too, Dr Benjamin. You're not doing your daughter any favours by getting stressed. You need to save your strength.'

'You're right, Anna. That's good advice.'

'She does important work. It's great there are still idealists around.'

Anna remembered why she had rung. 'Perhaps we should save a psychiatric study of mankind for another time. Then I can tell you about the crazy dreams I've had. I dreamed I was my own great-grandchild and saw myself as a great-grandmother . . .'

'I think that's for the best, Anna. But thank you for ringing.'

'I'll be sure to follow the news, Dr Benjamin.'

'Benjamin . . . or Dr Antonsen.'

'OK, Dr Antonsen. I mean, Benjamin! I should have read your card a bit more carefully.'

'Take care.'

'You, too. I'll be thinking about you.'

A Winter's Night

She is sitting under a glittering sky by a small clearing in the forest. She is holding the terminal in her lap, discovering exactly what happened to her planet. She wants to see the destruction. This is why she has gone to the forest. She wants to see the world falling apart. She feels ashamed of wanting to watch this, too ashamed to do it in her little room at home. Someone might come in and catch her. *You're going to have to stop feeling sorry for yourself, Nova!*

She stares at the screen, flitting around the world from one point of no return to the next. She finds everything she is searching for. There is no shortage of apps which document the earth's decline. The planet is under surveillance: the terminal shows glaciers advancing and drought spreading across

Africa, America, Australia and the Middle East. The truth is four-dimensional. She sees nature as it was, fertile and varied, in dazzlingly sharp relief. But then the image changes and destruction sweeps across the screen. She sees continents, countries and regions being robbed of their species and their allure. It is incredible that these worlds are at her fingertips but, as her fingers dance across the screen, she realises it is a macabre dance.

She has access to all the world's news programmes, reports and documentaries. Apps allow her to define what she is looking for with even greater precision. She has access to everything. The planet has no borders now. Her knowledge has no limits. Everything is online and she is hooked.

She zooms in and out. The terminal is a time machine. Impressions crowd her senses. The terminal has good speakers and her ears carry messages to her soul. Not only can she watch the rainforests come down; she can also hear the chainsaws. She can see them being consumed by fire and hear the crackle of the hungry flames. While she watches terrifying clips of hurricanes and cyclones, she can hear the water splash, the winds howl and the people scream.

She watches intently as the world's population is

decimated, as millions starve or perish in natural disasters or in desperate wars for what is left. No census has been taken since the catastrophes began. But it is estimated that the world's population is well under one billion.

The landscapes she wanders through are not imaginary. She has to remember to keep account of the app's two coordinates: time and space. The Amazon in the year 1960 is not the Amazon in the year 2060. The Serengeti in 2080 is not the Serengeti in the year 1980. The earth in 2082 is not the same as in 2012.

Anno Anna is not anno Nova. The time is no longer five to twelve. It is twelve . . . twelve.

She flicks back one last time to the world as it was, to the endless rainforests, the savannahs and coral reefs. These perfect eco-systems are a thing of the past. That is why it is so heartbreaking to see them in their former splendour. It is as if she is looking at a different planet, not her own dry, barren earth.

She bursts into tears. She switches off the terminal and for a second everything around her is pitch-black. But high above in the vaulted sky, thousands of distant suns prick tiny holes into the night. She looks up at the broad belt of stars in the Milky Way.

The sky is full of suns like her own. But they are so far away they don't concern her. She finds no solace in them.

Perhaps intelligent life exists only on her planet. But what if, one day, there are no humans left? Will the stars and planets live on, with no one to look at them?

She pulls herself together and forces herself to stop crying. She decides to be sad no longer. She will not allow the people who destroyed her planet to take pleasure in the fact that she is crying; that she is sad.

The World's Inheritance

Anna went online and read about the hostage situation. But no new reports had emerged from the Horn of Africa. She watched a short news programme on TV. It had been broadcast that morning but she could download it easily – she was getting used to her new phone. Soon she found the Norwegian Broadcasting Corporation podcast and played a lecture she had listened to on the radio a few days before.

Modern man has predominantly been formed by our cultural and historical conditions, by the very civilisation that has nurtured us. We say we share a cultural heritage. But we are also formed by this planet's biological history. We also share a genetic heritage.

The earth existed for billions of years before mankind came along. It does in fact take a few billion years to create a human being. But will we survive the third millennium?

What is time? Time can be seen from many perspectives: firstly, the perspective of the individual, then that of the family, then that of culture and written culture, and then what we call geological time. We descended from tetrapods that crawled up from the sea at least 350 million years ago. Ultimately, we live on the axis of cosmic time. We live in a universe which is around 13.7 billion years old.

But these periods of time are, in reality, not as distant from each other as they might seem at first sight. We have every reason to feel at home in the universe. The planet we inhabit is exactly a third of the age of the universe, and the animal kingdom we belong to, the vertebrates, has existed for ten per cent of the lifetime of the earth and this solar system. The universe is no more infinite than this. Or, to put it another way, this is how deep our roots extend into the soil on which we stand, and how deep our kinship is.

Man is perhaps the only living creature in the whole universe that has a universal consciousness – a prodigious sense of this immense, mysterious cosmos of which we are an essential part. So maintaining life on this planet is not only a global responsibility; it is a *cosmic* responsibility.

We have every reason to feel at home in the universe! This was the sentence which had caught Anna's attention when she heard the lecture for the first time. Whether or not intelligent life existed elsewhere, life on Earth represented the whole universe to mankind. And, with the gift of consciousness, mankind was in a unique position. But mankind would not have been able to exist without other life forms. We could not exist without certain small bacteria. So these bacteria had a cosmic significance, because they contributed to man's consciousness. So let's hear it for the microorganisms! They could hardly have realised it, but they too have played a cosmic role!

Anna laughed. The notion that tiny bacteria

could contribute to giving the universe *meaning* made her chuckle.

She glanced back down at the petrol station and looked out at the gleaming winter scene. Now she really would have to call Jonas! But he beat her to it.

Jonas lived further up the valley, in Lo. They hadn't met before she started at her new school that previous autumn. The school was attended by children from half the county, and they lived kilometres apart. That was one of the reasons it was so difficult for them to meet in the evening.

This year, skiing conditions had been good since the middle of November, and Anna and Jonas had begun to meet in the mountains, in a cabin which had belonged to Anna's family for generations. And that was exactly where Jonas suggested they meet later. He said it was his last chance to see his fifteen-year-old girlfriend.

That didn't go down well with Anna because it reminded her of the letter Nana had written to her great-grandchild. It must have been written before 12.12.12. Otherwise it wouldn't have appeared when she applied the search filter.

'Actually, I'm a bit busy. With stuff,' she said.

'With something important?'

'Yes, Jonas. But there's something else as well. Have you read the news today?'

'I have. You took so long to call me, I went online. Why?'

'Ester Antonsen.'

'The woman in Somalia?'

'Yes.'

'I can barely believe it. She'd only just landed.'

'Ester Antonsen is Benjamin's daughter. I've just spoken to him on the phone.'

'You spoke to Dr Benjamin?'

'His name's Antonsen, Jonas. Benjamin Antonsen. I misread his name.'

'So he rang you out of the blue to say his daughter had been kidnapped?'

'No, I rang him.'

'Why?'

'Never mind why. I wanted to ask his professional opinion about why we're destroying our planet. But perhaps I rang because I'd just seen a picture of Ester. It must have reminded me of a photo Benjamin had in his office. But the photo turned out to be of Benjamin's wife, when she was young. They look so alike . . .'

'Anna – we can talk about this in the mountains . . . Are you coming?'

She pretended to need persuasion. '. . . I'll come on one condition.'

'What?'

'I need you to help me solve a problem.'

'Go on. I'd do anything for you.'

'How can we save 1001 species of plants and animals?'

'What? Is this something to do with the pressure group?'

'Not directly. But I have to clear something up . . . something I dreamed, Jonas, something I dreamed last night.'

'Oh, Anna. But why 1001? Why so precise?'

She laughed. 'It's a nice number. A bit like *One Thousand and One Arabian Nights*. Children say a thousand when they mean lots and lots. But I'm saying 1001.'

'You're crazy.'

'Maybe. I'm a bit worried about that. But Benjamin gave me a clean bill of health . . .'

'We'll have to trust him then.'

'When we meet, tell me how we'll save 1001 species of plants and animals from extinction, OK? If you can do that, I love you. And if you can't, I'm going to dump you!'

'I'll do it then. I don't want you to dump me.'

'I doubt I could, Jonas. I love you too much.'

'See you in the cabin.'

'Hang on!'

'Yes?'

'Do you believe in parallel universes?'

'Anna!'

'It's back. I feel like I'm living in two different worlds. Or at least that I have links with another world. That there's something on the other side . . . and it's sending me a message.'

'We've talked about this before.'

'I know.'

'It frightens me when you talk like this.'

'What are you frightened of? The fact there's another dimension or of what's on the other side?'

'I'm frightened of what's going on in your head.'

'There's no need, Jonas. See you in a bit.'

'Take care. And please try to focus on this world, on our world – all right?'

'OK. I'll try. See you soon!'

'See you.'

As Anna stood there thinking, it happened again:

she remembered another snippet, an everyday
scene from another life, a thousandth of another
universe . . .

The Balloons

She comes into the garden with a bunch of red helium balloons, each showing an extinct animal. She walks down to the staging post to sell them because she is saving up for a new terminal. Many travellers will buy a lion or gorilla balloon for their children, she thinks.

In the garden her mum and dad are both on step-ladders, hand-pollinating the fruit trees. Bees are a thing of the past. Their numbers started to fall a hundred years ago, for a variety of reasons. Then, all of a sudden, they died out completely. Now people have to do by hand the painstaking work performed by billions of bees.

Her mum and dad wave to her from their ladders. Both are wearing blue overalls. She thinks how beautiful her mum is, and how handsome her dad looks.

'Nice balloons,' says her dad.

'It's almost a shame to sell them,' her mum adds.

Nana comes into the garden carrying a big tray. She has made a casserole. Nova knows the food is synthetic. She is sick of all this synthetic food even though she is told it contains all the nutrients she needs.

Nana asks for help setting the garden table, which has already been adorned with a vase of red tulips. She walks towards Nana to take something from the tray. She tries to move the balloons from her right to her left hand. But for a fraction of a second her concentration slips and she lets go of the balloons. It happens so quickly.

For no more than a quarter of a second she loses her grip on the strings and the balloons rise an arm's length above her head, still so near that she could *almost* jump up and catch them. She jumps and grabs at them, but she is a tiny bit too late, and the balloons continue to rise, dispersed by the wind, now shrinking red dots against the blue sky.

The Swimming Pool

There were two possibilities. Either, Anna had simply dreamed up the distant future which she'd seen the night before – a whole chain of colourful episodes had been queued up, like pearls on a string, from the moment she went to bed to the moment she woke up. Or else she had been plucking her dreams from this same universe for a long time, but this was the first time she had remembered them all. The dream about Nana and the red ring was definitely from last night because she had woken up during it, and perhaps that dream had rescued all the others from a sea of oblivion.

Which of the possibilities was more likely? And which made more sense?

But perhaps there was a third possibility, and

Anna was not ready to rule it out: everything she had dreamed might have been true. Perhaps she really *did* have a great-grandchild far in the future, a miracle child who, in some magical way, transmitted her thoughts to her great-grandmother when that great-grandmother, Anna, was a girl herself. There was so much in nature that we didn't understand. Time, for example. What is time?

One thing was sure though: Nova's mum and dad, who had been hand-pollinating the fruit trees, had looked nothing like her own parents. They didn't look like anyone Anna had ever met.

She couldn't recall ever having seen a woman as beautiful as Nova's mother, not even in films. She had never met a man as handsome as Nova's father, either. The glint in his eyes was unforgettable. Anna would have walked a hundred miles to set eyes on him again.

Either she was psychic and the people she had seen in her dreams were real and would live at some point in the distant future. Or she had created two very special individuals from nothing more than her imagination. It was very fertile, after all. But which option was more exciting? Perhaps she was the one who had *created* them!

If she were arty she could have drawn Nova's parents' faces down to the very last detail. If she saw them in the street she would recognise them instantly and go and say hello. One of them – either the mum or the dad – could have been Anna's grandchild!

Again she was reminded of the letter Nova had found online, the letter Nana had written when she was a young girl. But that was Anna, of course! She felt giddy as all the connections dawned on her, as she thought about consciousness and dreams.

But what *was* consciousness? And what were dreams?

While she was in the bathroom, she remembered one time that spring when she had gone down to the garden. Mum had been walking around with a very long measuring tape. Anna asked her what she was doing, and Mum said they were maybe going to dig up the garden and get a swimming pool. It wasn't that expensive, she said, the estimate was much cheaper than she or Dad had imagined.

At first Anna just gaped in amazement. Then she wondered whether her mum had taken leave of her senses. There was no room in the garden for a swimming pool. But Mum insisted there was *plenty* of room for a pool, and she knew because she was measuring it. Of course they would have to dig up the fruit trees. And the roses and the redcurrant bushes. There was also a bee hive in the tiny garden, but Dad had decided to stop beekeeping ages ago.

'The summer's so short, Anna. It's nice to have a refreshing swim when it's hot. And it'll be good exercise.'

There was a white bench on the lawn, and some garden chairs. Anna beckoned her mother over and told her to sit down. She did as she was told and Anna sat down on the chair opposite so she could look her mother in the eye.

'Has your *estimate* factored in the benefits of a garden? What about all the pears and plums we'll lose? What about all the cherries and redcurrants and roses?'

A garden wasn't only there to look nice, she said. A garden was a home for nature. But at the same time, she loved the elegant lawn – with its red and white clover – just the way it was. She loved walking around in the garden and being part of it and, in case her mum hadn't noticed, she still loved climbing the pear tree.

'I'm happy here,' Anna said.

The swimming pool was never talked about again.

The Tulips

She is walking along the river with a bunch of red tulips which she has probably bought from the shop.

Suddenly she hears loud bangs on the other side of the river. She crosses the bridge and can hear rhythmic blows coming from the pine forest on the ridge of the hill. She sees one tree fall. And then another.

She follows a narrow path to the top, where the banging is loudest, and sees a group of men in blue uniforms. They are striking the trees with axes. There are maybe twenty men in all. They tower over her: they look as though they're two metres tall and weigh one hundred kilos.

One of the men is wearing a red fez. He must be

the foreman. She walks over to him and peers up into his cheery blue eyes. He rests his axe on the ground.

'What's going on?' she asks.

The man wipes sweat from his brow. 'We're cutting down the forest.'

'Why?'

He laughs, and she thinks her question must have sounded naïve. But the man is not unfriendly.

'They're going to build a wind farm here. And so the forest has to be cleared. You win some, you lose some, young lady. That's how the world works.'

'I think it's a shame to lose the forest.'

He laughs again and looks at the red tulips. 'But perhaps that's not the point.'

'What do you mean?'

'Ask me how long it will take us to complete this job?'

'How long will it take you to complete this job?'

He raises his thumb to the sky. 'It's early spring now, there are twenty of us and our axes are sharp. I reckon we can do this by Christmas.'

She nods. 'Merry Christmas to you then!'

She passes him the tulips and adds: 'Here you go. I believe they're for you.'

The big man bows respectfully.

'Thank you very much. Shall I tell you what the funny thing is?'

She is confused. She looks up into his big blue eyes and nods.

'If I had a can of petrol and a chainsaw, I could have done this job in a couple of days on my own.'

The Ignition Key

As Anna turned to go she caught sight of the two boxes: *What is the world?* and *What has to be done?* She put all the print-outs and cuttings into plastic sleeves and squeezed them into the pocket of her blue anorak, along with her phone. Soon she was on her way to the petrol station. She carried skiing poles in her left hand and the skis over her right shoulder.

A car idled in front of the carwash with its engine running. As Anna stuck her skis into the snow at the roadside, a woman in a yellow cape marched towards the car. She had a hot dog in one hand and a magazine in the other.

'I was just about to turn off your engine and throw the key into the snow!' Anna shouted. Then she threw on her skis, and with that she was gone, heading into the mountains.

We're destroying our planet, she thought. *We're the ones doing it, and we're doing it in plain sight.*

A few days ago she'd had an extra key cut so Jonas could let himself into the cabin if he arrived before she did. She wondered who would get there first today. He had eight kilometres to cover while she had only five. But Jonas skied faster than she did. She had given him a lot to think about but she doubted that would slow him down. It would probably speed him up. The faster you think, the faster you ski. And vice versa: the faster you ski, the faster you think.

While Anna skied she thought about the hostage drama in Somalia and the strange conversation she'd had with Benjamin. Before she set off she had looked at the headlines and Googled news from Somalia. She had read that foreign fleets caught a lot of fish off the coast and that might be a factor in the piracy problem. Boats, from the EU no less, had been fishing illegally in Somali waters for a long time, bringing in catches worth several hundred million dollars a year. Somalia had asked the UN to use its anti-piracy warships to combat illegal over-fishing by foreign boats ... She read that Somalia was protesting against Kenya's plans to drill for oil off Somalia's coast. According to the UN's Convention on the Law of the Sea, many of the areas in question belonged to Somalia. Four major oil companies were involved, among them Norwegian Statoil. But there was no news of the hostages, only an article which said no ransom demands had been made so far.

Anna reached the higher farms with long, gliding movements. When she reached the last farm she stopped for a moment, hypnotised by the sight of a green postbox. Hadn't she dreamed about green postboxes? Or had she dreamed about machines? She couldn't quite remember what that dream had been about. But perhaps her dreams would come back to her as the day went on. It was barely twelve o'clock.

She reached the Lia Forest, where Nova had sat with her under the stars. She stopped to catch her breath, clutching her ski poles and smiling to herself.

Anna had a secret hiding place, a natural clearing which was almost free of light pollution in winter because it was sheltered from the village and the slalom run. She could stand in complete darkness, looking into the night – just as Nova had done.

Planet Earth was more breathtaking than all the things in the sky put together. Wasn't a squirrel more remarkable than a black hole? A hare or a fox meant more to her than a dead supernova.

But Anna didn't only go into Lia Forest at night. Once, not long ago, she'd had an argument with Jonas and had wanted to be alone. They'd fallen out over her 'visions', and she had been so fed up afterwards that she'd run away to the woods.

She had never seen a soul in that space between the trees. But she had seen deer. She had always thought deer were more mysterious than humans. They had no job to go to. They didn't go to school, and they never had homework. They didn't have to think about houses or religion or taking out insurance. They didn't have names or an ID number, and they belonged to no one. They just *were*. And yet: they were no less soulful for that.

How would it feel to be inside the head of a deer? Would it feel different from being in the head of a camel?

In the dream, Nova had been sitting in the same clearing. No, she hadn't *sat* there. She *would* sit there with her terminal seventy years from now. Anna wasn't sure it was a coincidence that Nova had chosen the same special place as Anna had. Maybe Nana had taken her there once. Anna decided that if she ever became a great-grandmother to a girl called Nova, she would show her this very clearing . . .

She realised her thoughts were going round in circles, and she laughed. She laughed so loudly that she frightened ptarmigans from the shrubs. Soon she set off again, and a quarter of an hour later she was up on the plateau. The gigantic mountain lay bathed in winter sunshine, its bare rock face looming ahead.

The Paths

It is late autumn and she is wearing a red scarf. She is following a narrow path towards the old farm. The steep hills lie behind her – she has already reached the plateau. The birch trees are dense here too. She knows that this area was once bare rock, but now the land is covered with birches and willow thicket. And here, deep inside the vegetation, she can see neither the rock nor the icy mountains. She knows that the highest peaks are covered in moss and lichen; she knows about those mountains the way she knows about legends and myths. Perhaps one day she will know the wilderness well enough to navigate its paths and gravel tracks, but for now she cannot detect them.

She loves walking between the silver trunks. The

leaves and heath shine bright red and yellow – and this year there is a carpet of blueberries and cowberries on the forest floor.

She steps lightly, as though she is floating a few millimetres above the ground. The path she is following crosses another. Without pausing to think she changes direction – the cabin can wait till another time.

She is almost ashamed of how much she is enjoying this walk. The fact there is birch forest here means the mountain's native flora and fauna are gone. The traditional mountain scene – with grazing cows and sheep and goats – has been lost. A price has been paid for the forest's labyrinth of paths, and that price is drought and hunger in other parts of the world.

But she is attached to this landscape. It is where she belongs.

She comes to a red sentry box. A uniformed soldier is standing erect by a solid boom barrier. She is surprised, but not very much, for this is her forest and she knows the forest's rules.

The soldier wants to inspect her terminal. She gives in and passes him the device. He wakes it up and flicks furiously. It is as though he has gone through hundreds of websites in seconds. But then he hands the terminal back to her, opens the barrier and lets her pass.

The Mountain Farm

Anna unlocked the door to the cabin. It felt damp and cold so she lit the wood burner and put on water for tea.

Sometimes, when she came here on her own, she would get the sense she was with invisible friends. She would hear a buzz of voices in her head. And if she was in the right mood, she would shout back: 'No, I don't agree with you on that!' or, 'Exactly! I've *always* thought that!' She would shout so loudly she would frighten the birds on the drive. If anyone had come in they would have thought she was talking to herself. But she was never afraid of what was happening.

Suddenly she heard herself shout: 'Ester! How is Ester?'

Anna grabbed her smartphone from her pocket. The coverage was good. She clicked on her favourite paper and now there *was* news:

BREAKING NEWS: The American and Egyptian hostages have been released from captivity in Somalia and have successfully crossed into Kenya, where they are being looked after by the Kenyan authorities and staff from the UN's World Food Programme. Only the Norwegian aid worker, Ester Antonsen, remains in captivity . . . Sarah Hames and Ali Al-Hamid (pictured) have passed on the kidnappers' demands: in order for Antonsen to be released, Statoil must guarantee that they will not participate in Kenyan-led oil explorations in Somali waters . . . Hames and Al-Hamid describe the kidnappers as professional and determined men who view the drilling as illegal . . .

Anna didn't need to read any more. She rang Benjamin. He picked up after a few seconds:

'Ben! Anna here. How are you?'

'I can't stay on the phone long.'

'Are you getting the help you need?'

'I need to *give* help as well. Ester has a husband and children.'

'Is there anyone with you now?'

'Not at the moment. But the Foreign Office are calling me with updates.'

'And no one's heard from Ester directly?'

'No, no one. What worries me most of all is how *she* is.'

'Of course.'

'Ester's been claustrophobic ever since she was small. Do you know what that means?'

'She's afraid of confined spaces.'

'And I wasn't able to cure her. Me, the psychiatrist. When she's in New York she'll climb up forty flights of stairs so she doesn't have to take the lift. I've got to go, Anna. I've got to get off the line.'

'Hang on!'

'Quickly then!'

'Stay strong. Try to *repress* any negative feelings. Take your mobile and go on a nice long jog.'

'You're a strange child, Anna. But thank you!'

More to keep herself busy than anything else, Anna took the cuttings from her pocket and spread them out on the table: *What is the world?* at one end and *What has to be done?* at the other.

She didn't move too far from the window so she could see Jonas approaching. Up here on the slope she had an unobstructed view for kilometres to the south-west. This is the direction he would come from, but she couldn't detect any movement, not even at the furthest edge of her vision, on the steep crust of snow he would have to cross to reach her.

The sun was low in the sky even though it was the middle of the day. It was a few days before the winter solstice. The sharp light was coming through the window horizontally, and dazzling her.

She hoped Ester wasn't lying in a dark room with her hands tied behind her back and her head pressed down on the ground, even though that was precisely the scene Anna was imagining. She pushed these thoughts to one side and decided to believe Ester's kidnappers were treating her well. She hoped that Statoil would soon give the guarantees the hostage-takers had demanded. If not, she would organise a demonstration the next day with the people from her pressure group.

One of the cuttings on the table was about belief and hope. It had been in the *What is the world?* box.

According to current theories, the universe came into existence approx. 13.7 billion years ago. The event is widely known as 'The Big Bang'. But the birth of the universe was not necessarily the beginning of all things. The Big Bang may have been more of a transition from one state to another.

No one can explain what is 'beneath' or 'behind' the universe. It is the ultimate riddle. No one can blame us for simply ceding to its mystery.

To look out into the night is to recognise the limits of our intellect. Beyond these horizons there are boundless opportunities for faith and belief . . .

We have the capacity for belief, and for hope that our world will be saved. But we cannot be certain that a new Earth and a new sky are waiting for us. It is doubtful whether supernatural powers will ever bring about a Judgement Day. One day, though, we will be judged by our own heirs. If we forget to consider them, they will never be able to forget us.

To look out into the night is to recognise the limits of our intellect . . . Perhaps looking out into the night was like looking into your own mind. Anna reckoned it was just as mysterious. But could there be a connection between the riddles in the corners of her mind and the riddles of the universe?

Climate Quotas

The rain is pelting down. She is wearing high
heels and walking under the large red umbrella. She is only going to the shop, probably to pick
up something for lunch. There have been shortages
recently.

In front of the shop a little stall has been set up. It
is the first time she has seen anything like that here.

The man behind the stall has white hair and
wears a grey smock. His table is covered with glossy
catalogues. As she approaches she realises they must
be old travel brochures. They look brand new, but
she knows they are from the olden days. No one
prints catalogues like that any more.

A blue pennant hangs from the awning of the
stall. It says: Cheap climate quotes.

She picks up one of the catalogues and looks at inviting pictures of white beaches and startlingly blue swimming pools. The white-haired man smiles cheerfully. She has the biggest umbrella of anyone, and he is obviously impressed.

'Wouldn't a bit of sun be a fine thing, young lady? The quotas are here.'

She puts down the catalogue, points to the table and says: 'They must be at least forty years old.'

'You're quite right.'

'You don't sell real trips so I don't need real quotas.'

He looks at her in surprise, in annoyance almost:

'Who says the quotas have to be real? You know as well as I do the whole thing's a charade.'

He tears a form off his pad, takes a red felt pen from his pocket and asks: 'What's your name?'

'Nova.'

'Surname?'

'Nyrud.'

He writes down her name then hands her the form:

1 – one – climate quota. Nova Nyrud is hereby entitled to purchase carbon emissions totalling

one tonne, the equivalent of a flight for two to Alicante or Naples.

She studies the form and looks up at the man again.

'But I don't want to go anywhere.'

'That's why I gave you this quota for free. If you'd really intended to release a tonne of CO_2, you'd have had to pay for it. Pollution comes at a cost.'

'Of course . . .'

'But now you understand the rules of the game. You can travel wherever you like – with the cleanest conscience in the world – if you buy climate quotas based on how far you're going. The arithmetic is pretty basic.'

She doesn't understand the logic. 'Do you mean I can travel without polluting if I just buy climate quotas?'

The man nods emphatically. 'Your flight would be *climate neutral*, and that's much nicer than *climate negative*. And just for a hundred or two.'

The photos catch her eye. She is tempted by the palm trees and the beaches. In some of the pictures she can read 'cheap', 'cheapest' and 'best winter offer'. She looks up at the man and says: 'Then I'll buy twice as many climate quotas as I need. Won't it be just *great* for the climate if I go travel-crazy?'

She can see the man thinking this through. Then he nods and says authoritatively: 'According to the calculations, your travel will be *climate positive*. The more you travel, the better it will be for the environment. A few weekends away, here, a few longer breaks, there, hey presto, you've contributed to sucking an apportioned quantity of climate gases from the atmosphere. And you get all the tax-free deals thrown into the bargain. Okay, my dear. I think you won this round.'

She turns on her heel, tipping over the enormous umbrella and sending a cascade of water over the table and the catalogues. She doesn't know whether she did this by accident or on purpose. But she bows in apology to the man with the white hair and sends another stream of water over all the catalogues.

'Sorry! It's our bloody climate!'

Another Chance

Anna was back at the window. She spotted what looked like a tiny red louse approaching in the distance. But she was blinded by the December sun. She picked up her binoculars and went to the front doorstep. Yes, that was Jonas in his red ski suit! No one skied like he did.

Ten minutes later he was standing in front of her, panting. It was still so cold on the porch that his breath came out in white clouds. She took off his blue peaked cap and ear-warmers, put her arm around his neck and kissed him. Jonas pulled her to him, but he was still gasping for air.

'Have you . . . been here . . . a while?' he asked.

'Just long enough for me to start missing you. So quite a while . . .'

'Were you here by yourself?'

She laughed. 'Yes, Jonas. I don't have any invisible friends with me today, and I haven't met any goblins or trolls.'

He was still out of breath. 'Heard . . . any more . . . about . . . the hostage?'

Anna found the web page and passed the phone to him.

'I've spoken to Benjamin. He's really worried. But I think I managed to cheer him up a bit.'

'How?'

'I suggested he went jogging. It won't solve his problems, but it won't create any new ones, either.'

Jonas had his breath back now. He walked over to her, put his hands on the back of her head and kissed her properly.

'Anna,' he said. 'I've always thought you would make a good psychologist.'

She looked up at him. 'Always, Jonas? All three months of always?'

'Time's got nothing to do with it. I feel like I've known you for ever.'

He took his hands from her head but kept looking into her eyes. She loved it when Jonas stood staring into her eyes. Sometimes he did it for so long that one of them would giggle, and then the other would burst out laughing, too.

He looked at the cuttings and print-outs spread across the table. Anna was responsible for collecting information for the pressure group, and this was the first time she had shown him her work.

'I wonder what *you've* brought with you,' she said.

He smiled enigmatically, and Anna had a sense he wasn't going to disappoint her.

'Shall I tell you why I gave you that task?'

'You dreamed something last night?'

He tried to hug her, but she stiffened. She had to get the words out.

'I woke up from a crazy dream, and it had something to do with the task I set you and what's in these papers. But it also had something to do with the drought in Africa. Are you following?'

'No, Anna, but don't let that stop you . . .'

He sank down on the long bench with his back to the window.

'I dreamed I was living several generations in the future,' said Anna, waving her arms. 'Oil had run out. Almost all the fossil fuels had been used up. The rainforests had been burnt down and the peat marshes had rotted. There was so much CO_2 in the air and in the sea. Our planet's resources had been destroyed and people were starving.'

Jonas looked up. 'Someone's been swotting up on their natural science . . .'

She was so happy to see him she didn't mind being teased.

'Hear me out, though. Tropical parts of the world had turned into deserts, and that meant there was even more CO_2 in the atmosphere. Thousands of species had died out and all the monkeys were gone. People had to *hand-pollinate* crops because bees had become extinct. Nature had been destroyed. Civilisation had almost broken down and the world's population was so much smaller than it is today. Then came the wars for resources and soon it was all over. The pockets of people who remained were silent.'

'The worst thing is that it could happen,' Jonas said.

She had laid out mugs and biscuits and went over to him with the teapot. He tried to pull her towards him again, but she freed herself with a smile and went back into the kitchen.

'Listen,' she said. 'In the dream I had this really cool tablet, a kind of terminal that could show all the films ever made. I could see everything that had happened to the planet in slow motion. I'd sit for hours studying plants and animals which had died out years ago.'

'Well that's happening already . . .'

'I felt so cheated, Jonas! It was like the earth had been hijacked. I lived with my mum and dad, and my great-grandmother, in the house I live in now. I had the same bedroom, except that in my dream it was painted blood-red. My name was Nova, and my great-grandmother was called Anna, though we just used to call her Nana.'

'Anna. Like you . . .'

She realised it was impossible to tell Jonas everything because a lot of the story depended on things she hadn't come to yet – things which, for logical reasons, she couldn't come to until she had told him what she was in the process of telling him.

'And she turned sixteen on exactly the same day I will. But this was 2082, and my great-grandmother was eighty-six years old.'

Jonas whistled loudly. 'Ah, I'm beginning to understand . . .'

'I had a very difficult relationship with my great-grandmother. Because even though I loved her

I still hated her for being part of a greedy generation that had *known* where we were heading but had done nothing to change course. I demanded that she gave me the planet back, as it had been when she was my age. And if she didn't, I would chase her into the forest. I would have been capable of murdering my own great-grandmother like the children in fairy tales who killed old witches and trolls.'

'Then you woke up?'

She shook her head. But what should she tell him next?

'You know the petrol station by my house? Well, that was gone, because there were no cars on the roads, apart from the big, white vans – I'll come back to them another time. But there were long caravans of Arabs with camels. They were crossing the mountains to Vestland, and they would stop to eat and rest where the old petrol station had been.'

'Arabs?'

'They were climate refugees. Their countries had been wiped out by sand. One of the boys was ill and we let him sleep in the cushion room until he was back on his feet. We called a doctor but it was my job to entertain him. We spent the days playing Ludo . . . When the boy finally had to leave he gave my great-grandmother a ring with a big ruby on it, and he called it a real Aladdin's ring . . .'

'How long did he stay in the cushion room?' Jonas asked. He seemed a bit concerned.

But Anna didn't answer. She was too busy trying to remember her dream.

'From that day on my great-grandmother always wore the red ring. And one morning she came into my room and announced that the world, and all its animals and plants, would get a second chance. I remember her touching the ruby – it was as though the new beginning had something to do with the ring. Then the room began to sway and she sat there chanting in this strange, creepy voice: *All you birds, be you so frail . . . come back . . .* Then I woke up, Jonas. It was only a few hours ago. I woke up and heard the birds outside. I woke up convinced it hadn't been a dream and my great-grandmother had done what she promised. The world had been given another chance, and all the animals and plants were back where they belonged.'

Jonas shook his head in disbelief. 'Wow. Even I'm beginning to believe your dream.'

'But that which was her responsibility in the dream is now *mine*. The roles have been reversed.

Now I'm the one who has to do something. And in seventy years' time I'll meet my great-grandchild. And if I haven't done my job, I'll be the one chased into the forest. If I can't help save the planet – then I'll have written my own epitaph.'

'This is getting a bit heavy,' Jonas said.

'I know but hear me out – there's more, because when I woke up *I* was wearing the magic ring, the ring I'd dreamed about.'

Jonas interrupted her. 'What did you say?'

Anna rolled up her sleeve, held her hand in the air and pointed to the ruby.

'Look! This is the ring my great-grandmother was wearing in the dream. This is the ring that allowed us to go back to the beginning.'

Jonas looked as though he didn't know what to believe.

'And you just woke up wearing it? Or were you wearing it when you went to bed last night?'

Anna nodded proudly. She told him she had been given the ring the day before. It had been a sixteenth birthday present, but because her mother was going to a conference in Oslo she had been given it two days early, along with her new phone.

'Because of the dream I've decided to wear the

ring for the rest of my life. That way I'll never forget what I have to do. And I'll still be wearing it when I become a great-grandmother. And if my great-grandchild is a girl I'll persuade her mum and dad to call her Nova. And then I can go into her room when she's sixteen and make sure she sees the ring. Only then will the circle be closed.'

'But if your dream comes true a lot of nature will also be lost. The planet will be destroyed.'

She shook her head.

'No, the world has been given another chance. That's the whole point. I've got the world back to how it was when my great-grandmother was sixteen. But I was only given this one chance.'

She looked down at the papers on the table, then glanced up at Jonas and said: 'That's why we have to get to work!'

The White Vans

Through the narrow window she catches sight of a white van. It has been a long time since she last saw one in the garden. She throws herself down the stairs, slips on moccasins and a winter coat, and rushes out.

In the garden she is met by her mother, who is on her way in with a bouquet of holly. The branches are dripping with red berries. Nova doesn't say where she is going. She knows that her mother doesn't like the white vans.

As she approaches, she sees people crossing the bridge. She isn't the only person keen to see what is on display. Soon she can read the large blue letters on the side of the van: World's Last Lemurs.

She knows that lemurs are strepsirrhine primates

from Madagascar, and she knows that Berlin is the only city to have housed them in recent years. Only when there is no hope that a dying species will manage to breed are zoos allowed to take the animals on tour. Lemurs have not been seen in the wild for many years.

She buys a ticket from a man with red, puffy cheeks and a black goatee. He is selling popcorn and candyfloss too, but she doesn't feel like either.

The ticket is the same size as a playing card. On one side there is a picture of a lemur with the caption *Lemur catta*. The other side says Animalia, Chordata, Mammalia, Primates, Lemuridae. There are a few sentences about why the species died out in Madagascar: their habitat was destroyed by fire, the trees were cut down to produce charcoal, and they were targeted by hunters. Global warming was the final nail in their coffin.

She is the first visitor to get into the van. A single cage runs the length of the interior and inside three lemurs jump between artificial logs and plants. The floor is covered with sawdust. The creatures are all females; it says on the ticket. She has often seen cards like this before. She has a whole pack of them. The cards remind her of the animals she managed to see before thcy disappeared.

The lemurs are a good metre long from their black snouts to the tips of their tails. Their black and white ringed tails are longer than their bodies. The animals swing nervously behind the netting and stare at her through yellow-brown eyes. She wonders how much they understand. She is sure they understand more than they can express. And she knows that in a year or two the IUCN app will beep a final farewell from this once so abundant species. As Nova leaves she sees a man holding two children by the hand. They are jumping up and down with excitement, holding buckets of popcorn. After they have seen the animals they might get some candyfloss too. It is not every day they are visited by the white vans.

The Frog

Anna went back online and read aloud: 'Break-ing news: Statoil denies that the company has plans to explore disputed areas off the Horn of Africa. For reasons of competition, they cannot comment on their activities in Kenya . . .'

'But they'll drill for oil . . .' Jonas said.

She looked at him imploringly. 'Right now that's perhaps not the point.'

'And what is the point?'

'Does this announcement help Ester Antonsen? Or Ben, for that matter?'

'Ben?'

'Benjamin. I'll text him.'

Any news?

A couple of minutes later, an answer arrived.

Nothing. I'll keep you posted.

Anna sighed. 'It must be awful for him.'

Jonas was rifling through the papers on the table. He picked up a print-out and read aloud:

Human nature is characterised by a horizontal sense of orientation. We scan our surroundings for potential dangers and prey. This gives us an innate ability to protect ourselves and our own. But we don't have the same aptitude for protecting our descendants, let alone species other than our own.

It lies deep in our nature to favour our own genes. But we don't have the same predisposition to protect our genes four or eight generations down the line. This is something we have to *learn*. This is something we have to learn the way we have learned to respect human rights.

From our origins in the Rift Valley we have fought a determined battle to extend our branch of the family. This battle has so far been won, for we are still here. But man as a species has been so successful that we are threatening our own existence. We have achieved so much that we are threatening the existence of all species.

We are cunning and vain primates, and it is easy to forget that, ultimately, we too are part of the natural world. But are we so vain that we prioritise our current lives over our responsibility for the future of the planet?

'That's a good question,' Jonas said.

'What is?'

Anna was thinking about a bigger question, the one she had asked him over the phone before they set off: how are we going to save 1001 species of animals and plants? But he pointed to the print-out he had just read from, and said:

'Are we so vain . . . ? I just said it was a good question.'

'That's why I printed it out.'

Anna was pleased Jonas liked the articles she had chosen. She was impatient to hear what he had come up with on the way to the cabin.

'So what do we do? How can we stop 1001 plants and animals becoming extinct?'

Jonas picked up another cutting:

To restore the planet's biodiversity, we would need a Copernican shift in our thinking. Living as though everything revolves around our time is as naïve as thinking that everything in the sky orbits the earth. But our time is no more significant than any time to come. Of course our time is most significant to us. But we can't live as if our era is the only one that matters.

Jonas nodded, at first to himself, but then he looked up and nodded to Anna.

'We laugh at the people who thought the earth was the centre of the universe. But is it any less stupid to live as though we've spare planets?'

Anna was becoming impatient. She couldn't wait to hear if Jonas had found a solution to her conundrum. But he picked up another piece of paper and read it aloud:

According to an old parable, a frog dropped in boiling water will immediately jump out. But if the frog is put into a pan of cold water which is gradually heated to boiling point, the frog won't sense the danger. It will die.

Jonas nodded again. 'Is our generation the frog?'

The Green Machines

She is in the capital with the boy who slept in the cushion room. So they have met up again. Nana has died, and now Nova is wearing the ring. She is so grown-up that she is wearing a black dress and a red shawl wrapped around her shoulders. She is dressed elegantly because she is visiting the capital, and she is wearing black because Nana is dead.

The boy has grown up too. He is wearing a white thawb which brushes the tarmac as he walks.

They walk through the city's main streets, stopping to gaze at the green machines. But the streets are still deserted. They have the city to themselves.

Green machines have been installed on every street corner, at all the underground stations and in front of important buildings.

The bells in the Town Hall tower chime a familiar tune. It is the signal they have been waiting for. They both go to the green machines, she with a red card, he with a blue one.

Their eyes lock and they smile before they swipe their cards. It is as though they are sharing a secret. She chooses which plants and animals she will pay for. Every time she types in a code, a video appears on the screen. The clips are only played if she has paid to help save that species.

The city begins to fill with people. They emerge from the underground stations, get off the buses and stroll down the streets. Many want to try the new machines. Soon the city is full of life, and queues form in front of the new attractions. People debate and gesticulate wildly.

Nova almost loses sight of her companion in the crowds. But luckily he is half a head taller than most. They meet again and high-five then she looks up at him and laughs.

'It's like the world's starting afresh.'

Game-ification

'The world has been given another chance,' Anna said, 'and now you must tell me how we should use that chance.'

Jonas looked up from the papers on the table and smiled the smile that Anna loved. He unzipped a pocket in his red ski suit, pulled out some folded papers and passed them to Anna.

She read the heading at the top of the first sheet: *How are we going to save 1001 species of plants and animals?* In smaller letters it said: *Answer to Anna's Question.*

She counted seven pages of type. 'I thought you were a bit late. How did you manage to write all this?'

'That's my secret. Just read it.'

Anna began to read aloud. As she did this Jonas

threw logs into the wood burner then peered out of the window with binoculars.

All plants and animals are dependent on their habitats, and when one part of nature is attacked it is a threat to all the species which thrive in that eco-system. What happens to these habitats is dictated by the economy. The rich stop at nothing to make themselves richer, by, for example, exploiting oil, coal and minerals in vulnerable regions. But the poor also exploit eco-systems in a way that cannot be sustained.

The problems are so big that people feel powerless. *What can I do to save the Amazon rain-forest? What responsibility do I have for the African savannah or Atlantic fish stocks?* People do not think like this. It's not how our brains work.

We are arrogant, selfish animals. In any attempt to save our planet we must use this as the starting point. Let me give an example.

If someone is particularly concerned by the fate of the tiger they might go out on to the streets collecting money for the Tiger

Foundation. They might organise a raffle or an auction or a jumble sale.

Almost everyone will give you a krone for the tiger without thinking twice. Some will give ten kroner, the price they'd pay for a bar of chocolate or a brownie. Some people will give a hundred kroner, and a few can afford a thousand kroner or ten thousand, especially if it means their name will appear in the newspaper. Perhaps there is a businessman somewhere who enjoys attention enough to donate half a million dollars. People pay that much for art. Sooner or later an old widow will leave the whole of her fortune to the Tiger Foundation, perhaps because her grandfather was a lieutenant in the British Army in India, and shot eight tigers, and one of the tiger skins is in front of the fireplace in the old family library in Birmingham.

People all over the world should be able to pay money into a particular account, let's call it the tiger account, and if a few million people regularly donate small amounts, in no time at all there will be billions of euros or yen to protect the tigers' habitats. Huge sums will have to be invested to stop illegal trapping and poaching not only of the tiger but also of its prey. This will require a whole army of forest rangers. The black market price for a tiger skin is half a million kroner, and the price continues to rise as the species dies out. The stricter the punishments for poaching become, the more the price rises. But penalties have to be made stricter still.

The forest ranger programme is only the first step, for then safe corridors have to be secured between the different stocks of tigers to prevent inbreeding, To secure populations of the tigers' prey – wild boar, deer and antelopes – the vegetation they eat needs to be conserved. To save the tiger you have to save a long list of plants and other animals. The tiger is a symbol of something much larger, and if the tiger disappears it is a very bad sign indeed.

'I see,' Anna said. 'But why the tiger? Why not the polar bear?'

'Ah. I'm just coming to that:

Why am I only talking about the tiger? What about the eagle owl or the Arctic fox? What about frogs and newts and all the other species under threat? Of course they should have their own accounts. Of course there can't just be a tiger programme: there has to be a thousand others. So there will 1001 foundations for threatened plants and animals. There are enough to *choose* from. Instead of sponsoring the tiger you can donate to the lion foundation or the newt foundation – whatever takes your fancy. The point is freedom of choice and all the *discussion* which goes with it.

Reports suggest that as many as a million species might be under threat because of global warming. But I don't think that a million different foundations is the way forward. One foundation for greenfly should be enough to attract the interest and generosity of those who feel attached to the greenfly. But if you want to save greenfly you'll have to save leaves, and by doing that you'll have saved hares and deer, and the lynx too. Everything in nature is interconnected. Biodiversity is as much about the tapestry of nature as the survival of individual species. Species which have lost their natural habitats and only survive in zoos are just one step away from extinction.

'I don't understand how you managed to write all this since we spoke on the phone.'

She looked up at Jonas, but he was still standing with his back to her scanning the plateau through binoculars.

'But what do you think?'

'I like it. I want to read the rest.'

'Carry on, then.'

My question is: how do we secure the broadest commitment to biodiversity? I have already mentioned freedom of choice as an important factor. Let me give another example:

Imagine taxpayers could choose what their taxes paid for? Instead of having to pay thirty per cent or forty per cent of their income, almost as a punishment, they'd have a direct influence on how their money was spent. How would that work? Would it cause chaos? Well, some would give all their money to defence, some to education, research, environmental conservation, foreign aid or public transport, and others would choose museums, nurseries, hospitals, opera or care for the elderly. But the end result might well be the same as it is now. The only difference would be happy taxpayers. This system would cater to individualism.

We can apply this idea to the environment. If the government introduced an environmental tax, many people would protest against yet another new tax. What do they mean by 'environmental' and what is the best environmental policy, they would say. If a more targeted tax were introduced to preserve the full range of plants and animals on Earth, more people might be persuaded, although some would argue about what our priorities should be. A sheep or reindeer farmer might not mind if the wolf or wolverine died out. City-dwellers would probably object to paying tax to save a snowy owl – when was the last time they'd seen one of those? Every taxpayer could select the species their money would go towards – there would be an element of personal choice. Then there would be something to discuss and feel *important* about.

Anna said:

'So you want 1001 different foundations? One day you stump up a krone or two for the bear foundation, the next you decide you have a soft spot for the golden eagle or the goshawk. And at least once a year, say, at Christmas, you set aside a krone or two for the newt or frog?'

'But which should come first: the goshawk or the frog?'

'The frog,' Anna said. 'The goshawk's got to have something to live off.'

'And before the frog?'

'Insects . . . and worms. I once saw a frog swallow an earthworm whole.'

'And before that?'

'Plants . . . fungus . . . and single-celled organisms.'

'OK.'

'But Jonas, I'm confused. You couldn't possibly

have written all this since you called me. I don't believe you!'

'Read on. Please.'

But I hear an objection. Are people really that bothered about nature? Haven't we turned the earth into a big theme park? Too many things are competing for our attention. We share a planet, but not everyone can think in terms of our planet. There is too much freedom in this world – the rich have too much disposable income, there are too many barrels of oil and private planes, and too little responsibility is taken for our planet and for the fair distribution of resources. It's so easy to get bogged down in other things. Just look at our newspapers and magazines: all they write about is sport and lotteries, restaurants and wines, cars and cruise ships, mobile phones and computers, gardening and interior design, cooking and fitness, medicines and lifestyle, health and drugs and alcohol, sex and the singleton . . . Not to mention gossip and scandal. Every single day a film star is getting married or divorced, going off the rails or ending up in rehab. This is what people talk about. This is what they want. No one cares about the natural world. Most people can reel off more footballers and film stars than they can species of bird.

Where am I going with this? I think the human factor will help us save 1001 species. We need to take human nature into account. We need to shift our attention from match results, celebrity gossip and the arts. We need to shift it towards our planet. Then the gossip columns can return, but they can mention the guillemot, puffin and the rhino too – not just Arsenal and Spurs. New lottery games can be introduced, based on threatened species: *Fancy a puffin ticket? Draw on 31 July. No, but I've got snowy owl scratch cards. And if you don't care about birds I've got some lynx tickets. The annual draw's tomorrow.* I can hear the buzz now. Finally, we're talking about nature: *No, I'm paying for the next round. I've just won a few kroner on the turtle . . .*

Her jaw dropped. But he had his back to her. 'Jonas . . . Jonas!'

Then he turned.

'You're mad!' she said. 'Absolutely wonderfully mad. Perhaps you should go to a psychiatrist. We could go back to Oslo. You could do with seeing Benjamin. Oh, I hope Ester's released soon.'

Jonas grinned, and Anna read on:

To achieve this we need an online catalogue with account numbers for every threatened plant or animal. International lotteries could be organised for families of threatened species like owls or cats or bears. There could even be bigger, biannual lotteries: for Carnivora, Anseriformes and Artiodactyla! They'd be on television! Celebrities would queue up to show off their outfits. Perhaps there could be some betting on population numbers in the breaks.

Do we have any reason to believe the world's population will be drawn to the glitz and glamour? If whole lunch breaks and evenings can be frittered away discussing how likely it is that eleven men can kick a ball into their opponents' goal more times than it ends up in their own, then it is not inconceivable that people might find it entertaining to think about how many lions or chimpanzees remain in the world, especially if they can win money, and perhaps some kudos, by doing so. Just imagine how much people could learn about nature from the publicity these games would attract. There would be a few lucky winners and some would get their five minutes of fame: *That guy's hot. He did best in all the animal sections. Now he's hit it big and bought a two-storey flat in Homansbyen.*

'No, Jonas. Now I think you've taken this too far.'

'You haven't finished.'

'You can't have written this today. Have you cut and pasted this from something?'

Jonas smiled. He didn't even try to answer her question.

You may be thinking I'm making a pact with the devil. But all I want is to make a pact with mankind. I think this scheme may generate a buzz. Grown-ups behave like children: they always have and always will. There has to be a competitive element because that is what humans like: *How many tigers remain? And where do they live? Quick now, otherwise you're out . . . And what do the present stocks need to survive? Ready? You've only got one chance . . . Exactly what can we do to bring back the tigers' habitats . . . Now put the tiger question into a global context. Teams . . .*

Wouldn't it be nice to read a different set of headlines? *Interior designer supports 114 vertebrates . . . Senior teacher Hjort leaves his fortune to the foundation for even-toed ungulates . . . Farmer in Vinstra has sold his smallholding and given all the proceeds to the lion . . . Woman gives her pension to the Arctic fox . . . Who has done most for bird stocks in the previous year? Excitement mounts before Sunday's TV ceremony for The Golden Bird . . .*

People will get something in return, something to put on their mantelpiece. If you give a thousand kroner to the reindeer you get a rosette. You can boast about it all you like: that's normal. People can sit at home and Google one another: *Did you know that he's got a black belt in saving reindeer?* That would make great water-cooler conversation.

'But I don't understand. You couldn't possibly have typed this up before you left. You were only fifteen minutes late – not ten hours. But you haven't mentioned climate change.'

'Keep going.'

But, I hear you say, what are we doing about climate change? Wasn't global warming the single most important threat to all those animals and plants? That's right, and that is why thirty-five per cent of all money raised goes towards wind turbines, solar energy, research into energy alternatives like fusion energy, and to reducing emissions – almost like VAT. Perhaps it is as easy as that. Reducing emissions is no longer a problem; it has become a part of the new national sport.

My aim has been to show that there is ultimately no point appealing to guilty consciences. If you have a billionth of the responsibility for the planet, what can you do? We cannot march in step. It is better to harness our interest in flora and fauna: in orchids and beetles, butterflies and budgies, finches and parrots, roses, redcurrants and rhododendrons, cats and dogs, snakes and iguanas, rats and mice. But when you give a few coins to the rose or the parrot foundation you are also slowing down global warming.

Finally, I would like to say a personal thank you to Anna Nyrud who inspired me to sit down at my computer and adapt this paper which I presented at school last Thursday. The title was 'How can we create nationwide commitment to biodiversity?'

Jonas Heimly, Saturday, 11.12.2012

Anna looked up. 'What did your teacher say?'

'She said it was entertaining. She said the language was fine and I read it well. I got a B and the only reason she didn't give me an A was because the conclusion was a bit "blue-sky thinking". The ideas were fresh, she said, but not quite grounded.'

'I was thinking something similar.'

They sat in silence for a few seconds.

'Hang on . . .' Jonas said, his eyes wide. 'Forget the catalogues and all the stuff about transferring money. I think I can see how it's going to work!'

'What do you mean?'

'The game.'

'Mm?'

'I can see green machines . . . All over the world . . . In airports, on street corners, at underground stations. All you have to do is swipe a card. You type in the code of the species you want to sponsor – a number from 0001 to 1001 – and then a video of that species appears on the screen. It's a kind of pay-per-view system. You see what you're sponsoring and at the same time you can play games to win money. It shouldn't be too difficult to design fun games about the environment. We could call it *game-ification* . . .'

Anna sighed. 'You've talked about this before.'

'No, I haven't! I just thought it.'

She sighed again. 'Then I must have dreamed it.'

There was a distant look in her eyes. She stared right through him.

'Anna . . .? Anna!'

Her eyes came back into focus. 'Sorry Jonas, I can't help it.'

Pretty Weekend Houses

S he has painted her nails red and is out walking in the birch forest. It feels silly to have painted her nails just before heading out into the woods. She never meets anyone there and she may have to use her hands.

She reaches a crop of trees and approaches the mountain farm. In the olden days this plateau was bare. Goats and cows lived on the land from Midsummer Night to September. There were pigs behind the barn and hens running around the yard. The sheep could take care of themselves all summer and roamed freely in the mountains. Now there is forest as far as the eye can see.

Traditional mountain dairy farming is not just out of fashion, it is now impossible. But the farmhouses still stand behind overgrown stone walls like small oases. Some of the buildings have been maintained and are used as weekend houses, and some families keep the old yards free of bushes and trees.

She lopes between the silver trunks and jumps over a tinkling brook. This forest has so many secrets, and she may be the only person who knows them. She hears a rustle in the brush and spots a deer. It must be a calf. For a second the animal stands perfectly still, eyeing her up. The next moment, it is gone.

She walks the last stretch to the old cabin. She had planned to go in, but when she is close she can see someone is already there. It is Nana. There is no doubt that it is Nana as a girl. She has seen so many pictures and videos of Anna when she was Nova's age. A boy is in the cabin too. He is also in his teens.

She creeps quickly past. She doesn't want to disturb them.

Aladdin's Ring

J onas reached across the table for her hand and stroked the ring. He said:

'Tell me about the ring.'

'In my dream? Or in the story about Aladdin?'

'No, in real life.'

She told him the ring had been in her family for more than a hundred years. Anna's great-grandmother was called Sigrid, and she had been given the ring by her Aunt Sunniva, an older sister who had emigrated to America and got engaged to a Persian carpet seller. It was a sad story, very sad, because only a few weeks after they had got engaged and Sunniva had received the beautiful ring, Esmail Ebrahimi, as her fiancé was called, fell from a paddle steamer into the Mississippi, and was never seen again. But maybe he didn't fall, maybe he was pushed overboard, because he was travelling with a whole bazaar's worth of Persian carpets, or at least a fair pile of them, and they vanished, each and every one, before anyone could report the salesman missing. Aunt Sunniva had had enough of America after that and returned to the 'old country' barely a year later. All she brought with her was this wonderful ring. And grief, so much grief, because Aunt Sunniva had fallen madly in love with the charming Persian, so madly that some people doubted the wisdom of the imminent wedding, and the relationship was said, in whispered tones, to be 'unbefitting'. But the ring was genuine enough. It was so mysterious and unique that, according to rumour, it once belonged to Aladdin, who appears in *One Thousand and One Arabian Nights*. In any case, that was what Aunt Sunniva said. She clung to this idea until the day she died of tuberculosis, as unmarried and childless as she had been when she came back from America. Her anguish at not having brought a child into the world haunted her until her dying day, and so she became more passionate about the family than anyone else in it. All she wanted was to mean something to the generations to follow. So she spent her days weaving and embroidering – she made the fairy-tale cushions which Anna's mum inherited. And then of course there was the red ring. It was indestructible and would pass down through the generations.

Jonas lifted her hand and studied the ruby more carefully. 'It really is beautiful ... I get the sense that it's very old, from a different age entirely.' He looked up at her. 'But do you think it could really be from the fairy tale? Wasn't Aladdin the one with the magic lamp?'

She nodded. 'Sunniva was just thirty-eight when she died of TB, and this ring was her only reminder of her great love. You don't give away such a special ring to just any woman, after all, or I can't believe you would. Esmail assured her it was more than a thousand years old.'

'He might have been laying that on a bit thick. She was a bit gullible, this aunt, wasn't she?'

Anna shook her head firmly. 'Fifty years ago it was examined by a Norwegian jeweller, a specialist in Oriental gems, and he confirmed that it was at least several hundred years old. He said it was an antique and perhaps should, by rights, be in the National Museum of Iran. He could determine with some certainty that the ruby came from Burma because it is the colour of dove's blood.'

'From Burma? Hardly from a fairy tale, then.'

'Esmail came from some sort of Iranian dynasty, and their family stories went back hundreds of years. Eight-hundred years ago there really was an Aladdin living in Persia. The name means "of noble faith", and he got this name, so the story goes, when he stood up to an evil sorcerer by saying his daily prayers and being true to his beliefs. The sorcerer wanted to kill Aladdin because he was wooing a beautiful girl. He managed to trick the sorcerer into giving him a magic ring, and the ring protected him from all the black magic the sorcerer tried to inflict on him.'

Jonas coughed. 'And this is the same Aladdin as the one in the fairy tale?'

Anna shook her head.

'Not necessarily. A Peer Gynt once lived in Gudbrandsdalen, but was he the Peer Gynt in Ibsen's play? I doubt it! And if I'm sitting here wearing a ring that once belonged to a real Aladdin living in Persia some point in the thirteenth century, I'm fine with that. By the way, if my oh-so-sensible mother is right, there may be another explanation.'

'Go on then,' Jonas said. 'I can do sensible.'

She looked him in the eye. 'It's not inconceivable that the ring really does come from someone called Aladdin. But he may have been named after Aladdin from the fairy tale. No one knows how old the story is.'

'I think I'm with your mother on this one.'

'But there was something else Aunt Sunniva told her family when she came back from America, you see, something she believed to her dying day. It all comes back to *One Thousand and One Arabian Nights*.'

Jonas looked at his watch, and she knew why. In a couple of hours it would be dark. But she went on: 'Twice this ring saved Aladdin's life. The first time was when he was held captive in a cave and rubbed his hands together to pray. A genie appeared and set him free. The second time was when his whole palace, with his wife and servants, was moved from China to Africa. Aladdin stood by the river, crazy with grief, and clasped his hands together in a final prayer before he drowned himself. But when he joined his hands, he touched the ring and the genie appeared for a second time, ready to reunite Aladdin with his beloved princess. The genie didn't have the power to undo everything that had happened and move the whole palace back to China – only the lamp could do that, and the lamp was in Africa – but the ring had the power to fulfil Aladdin's wish to be taken to the palace.'

'Yes, I remember that,' Jonas said.

'Aunt Sunniva always said this ring had the power to fulfil *three wishes*, and only two had been used up. She died convinced that whoever wore this ring could have a wish fulfilled, but only one. Sunniva never had a desire strong enough to justify using the ring's final wish, not even when she stared death in the face. At the time she thought it would be better to hand down this chance until there was such an immense, burning need that the ring could help to save the world.'

Jonas got up from the table and started pacing up and down. Eventually, he pointed at Anna and said: 'And you inherited this chance?'

She looked at him and nodded. 'But I've used it, Jonas,' she said, resigned but oddly triumphant. 'It's gone. I've used the last chance. Well, not yet, but seventy years in the future my burning wish will be for the world to be given a second chance. *That* wish was too great for the ring to fulfil. So instead I asked if *I* could go back in time to when the world still had a chance. And ta-da, here I am. Then I met you. And here we are, Jonas. We won't get another chance. There's no magic left in Aladdin's ring, I'm quite sure of that.'

Jonas shook his head. 'I don't know what to believe.' He sounded desperate.

'But perhaps that's not the main thing.'

'What do you mean?'

'The main thing is that you have to *believe*.'

Anna peered outside. She saw a girl about her age passing through the yard. She didn't quite catch the girl's face but there was something familiar about her movements.

She jumped up in amazement, then ran to the front door, opened it wide and shouted:

'Hello?'

Jonas went to the door to see who she had been shouting to.

'That was Nova,' she said, closing the door behind her. 'Didn't you see her?'

'I didn't see a thing.'

'She's the one I dream about. That's who I am when I dream.'

Jonas grabbed Anna firmly by the shoulder.

'You're not honestly telling me you saw your own great-grandchild walking past, are you?'

'Yes, I am!'

'But Anna . . .'

'Yes?'

'Why didn't you take a picture of her on your phone?'

She gave the question some thought. Then she said: 'Maybe that's not the point.'

'Isn't it?'

'The point is *I* saw her.'

The International Climate Court

I t is summer, and she is wearing a red dress. She
has been summoned as a witness to the International Climate Court at The Hague. It is the first
time she has been abroad.

She holds the boy's hand as they walk through the
town – they have become a couple, or perhaps they
are just pretending. He is wearing a dark suit and a
white shirt; he looks a little like a statesman. He too
has been summoned as a witness and perhaps that is
why he is wearing his best clothes. They could easily
be mistaken for a young married couple, but it is
probably just a game they are playing.

Between the tall buildings, they cross a large
square where a dozen camels are gathered. This
might have been a car park, once. There are still

some four-wheeled vehicles ploughing back and forth, but not many. The camels have been tethered to trees, and the vehicles are tethered to their charging stations.

Many years ago Norway was ordered by the International Climate Court to pay ninety-seven per cent of its Oil Fund towards initiatives such as the building of dykes and dams, and the fight against poverty. The emirate the Arab boy comes from received a similar sentence. The guilty are now paying for their actions. The rapid draining of fossil fuels was theft on a global scale, and Norway received an especially severe sentence because Statoil had extracted oil from tar sands and caused widespread pollution. In its defence the company said that if *they* hadn't done it *someone else* would have done it and probably caused more pollution. Now this was the defence every country used: *If we hadn't done it someone else would have.*

They walk up the steps to the huge courthouse where they will testify to the International Climate Court. Everyone's eyes are on them. Children throw rose petals on them as they pass; they have been mistaken for newly-weds.

In the gallery leading to the courtroom they are

interviewed by a TV company. They are asked why they have been called to give evidence. She looks into the camera and says:

'We're young. We have to testify that the climate crisis is not a conflict between nations. There's only one atmosphere and no national borders are visible from space. This is a conflict between *generations*, and the victims are young people today.'

She can feel the boy squeezing her hand. She isn't sure whether he is doing this because he agrees or because he thinks she is choosing her words well – or simply because they are both involved in a very important undertaking.

He looks into the camera and says:

'We both come from oil nations, and both our countries suddenly became very rich. But in the emirate where I am from we had to flee from the terrible drought and burning heat. We have no country any more – everything is just desert.'

Nova looks up at the boy and smiles. Then she looks into the camera again and adds: 'This young man is one of the many millions of climate refugees in the world today.'

The Ski Mittens

They started to tidy up the cabin. She closed the vent on the wood burner and he wiped the worktop. He asked whether he might go back with her and stay over. Or was the Arab boy still in the cushion room?

She giggled. Then she became serious. She took both of his hands in hers and looked into his eyes: 'Today's not convenient, Jonas. There's something I've got to do before I go to sleep ... something I have to write. I've got a deadline – there's something I have to send before I turn sixteen.'

She put all the print-outs and cuttings back into their folders, which she shoved into her pocket, and Jonas folded up his talk. He said:

'I wish I'd had a better answer to how we can save

1001 plants and animals. I shouldn't have used my talk from school.'

'I thought it was funny, Jonas.'

He put a hand on her shoulder and looked her squarely in the eye:

'I'm glad you didn't dump me.'

'I wouldn't have done that, Jonas. I want to be with you for ever.'

They skied down the hill, and when they reached the bottom, by Lake Brea, they said goodbye and prepared to go their separate ways, Jonas to the south-west and Anna to the south-east. Jonas was left wondering who she was writing to. Was it someone he knew?

But Anna was secretive and said she was writing to someone he might get to know one day.

Suddenly, something caught his attention. He pointed to her red ski mittens and said: 'When we arrived they were blue.'

She nodded mischievously.

'Where are they now?'

She held up her mittens:

'Here . . .'

He shook his head, but Anna took off her mittens and showed him how she could turn them inside out and wear them both ways. On one side they were blue, and on the other, red.

He hugged Anna, and said:

'Be careful on the slopes! And don't go looking for . . . for her. I'm frightened of losing you, Anna. Promise me that. Don't go . . . weird . . . on me.'

The Zoo

They are standing in an overcrowded tram on the way out of the city. It is hot. They are both wearing jeans and bright T-shirts. You can no longer tell that the boy comes from an emirate.

They get off the tram at the entrance to a big zoo. Over the gate there is a large red sign: The International Zoological Park. Admission is free. The International Zoo in The Hague belongs to all the people of the world and is on the UNESCO list of World Heritage sites.

As soon as they are inside they see vast expanses of savannah. Lions and tigers roam freely alongside antelopes and deer, insectivores and rodents, marsupials and apes. On first glance, you think they must be tame, but Nova knows these are not real animals.

They are holograms, and they are not made of flesh and blood but laser beams.

The colours, movements and shapes are incredibly realistic. Suddenly a kangaroo hops up in front of them, a black panther sprints through the grasslands and doves flutter through the air next to birds of prey. But they are not alive. They are virtual. They pose no threat to each other or to humans. For the same reason, they make no noise. They don't need to be fed or inspected for lice, and they don't defecate in the bushes.

He puts his arm round her shoulders. Walking through the zoo is like walking through the past; it is almost like being back in the Garden of Eden.

It was no accident that the World Government chose The Hague as the home of the International Zoo. It was set up in the same town as the International Climate Court as evidence of the habitats which had been destroyed. The living models for the animals in the zoo have vanished from the surface of the Earth, along with the terrain and the eco-systems in which they thrived. The vegetation in the zoo is also virtual. Many of the bushes, trees and shrubs are extinct. Only the grass they walk on is real, and when Nova bends down to tie her shoelace, she catches sight of a tiny greenfly, and *that* is perhaps alive, although it is difficult to tell.

A persistent jackal stands in their way, and the Arab boy tries to nudge it aside with his knee, but the dog is just a mirage.

He stops and lets the jackal slink past. He strokes her hair and runs his fingers through her auburn locks. Then he asks: 'Is this zoo here to give us pleasure or is it just an awful reminder?'

She puts her hands beneath his T-shirt, pats his chest and looks up at him. 'It's an unpleasant but necessary reminder – we must never be allowed to forget.'

Identity

Darkness had begun to descend. Anna skied through the birch trees and passed the car park. From there she continued down the mountain road, which hadn't been gritted.

Then she caught a glimpse of the girl she had seen up at the farm. The girl left the road and headed into the forest. She was carrying a machine under her arm, and it glowed with blue light. This time Anna managed to see her face. She looked a bit like – like Anna . . .

When she was dreaming that she was this girl, she hadn't seen her own face. She had never looked in a mirror. What bad luck!

She skidded to the side and trudged to where the girl had crossed the road. She continued into the clearing and saw deep footprints in the snow. But the girl had vanished into thin air.

Now it was almost dark, but not quite. There was no sign of a moon tonight, but more and more stars were appearing in the sky.

She had read somewhere that the closest star to the sun was 4.3 light-years away. It was called Alpha Centauri. Travelling at the speed of a jumbo jet, it would take five million years to get there.

Her own planet seemed so much closer and more vulnerable.

She remembered something she had read in an article from one of the red boxes. It talked about taking the plunge and daring to be more than you were. It was too dark to read now, and she didn't have a torch. She thought about the great-grand-child who had been in this same clearing with her terminal, and now Anna pulled off her mittens and took out her phone. She remembered one sentence in particular, and she Googled it to find the article online. *How far away is our ethical horizon?* It took less than a second for the article to appear.

How far away is our ethical horizon? Ultimately this is a question about *identity*. What is a human being? And who am I? If I was only myself – the body sitting here and writing – I would be a creature without hope. In the long run, that is. But I have a deeper identity than my own body and my short sojourn on Earth. I am a part of – and I take part in – something greater and mightier than me.

If I had the choice between dying at this moment, but with a guarantee that mankind would survive for thousands of years after me, or living in rude health until the age of one hundred, although the whole of humanity would die in the meantime, I would not hesitate. I would choose to die right here and now – and not as a *sacrifice* but because some of what I think of as 'me' is represented by the whole of mankind. And I am afraid of losing this part of me. Just the thought that it could happen scares the wits out of me. I am more frightened that mankind will be lost in a hundred or a thousand years than I am that my body might give up the ghost at any second – it will one day, whatever happens.

Sometimes I do think on behalf of the planet I inhabit. It is a part of me as well. I am concerned about the fate of this planet because I am frightened of losing the very core of my own identity.

It didn't say who the author of this article was, and Anna stood wondering who it could be. Was it a woman or a man? Then she had to laugh. The whole piece was about being something greater and mightier than one's self.

Perhaps that was why the author's name hadn't appeared!

The Planet

She is sitting in a spaceship with the Arab boy. They have won an international award recognising their efforts on the planet's behalf. The prize is twelve orbits of the earth.

There are just the two of them in the tiny cabin. They don't need to worry about anything technical: the shuttle is steered and controlled by computers; all they have to do is sit back and enjoy the trip.

They look down on their planet. Both of them have seen photos from the Apollo mission more than a hundred years ago. The globe is unrecognisable now. It is much more obscured by clouds and storms. This tallies with their experience on the ground. The planet that looked like a bluish-green marble now has more in common with a colourless ball of wool.

Despite all the clouds, it is still a spectacular feeling to be in space, and they can still glimpse some green, brown and blue patches between the cloud systems. *That's* Africa, and *there's* India, China and Japan . . .

What surprises her most is the silence. All she can hear is her friend's breathing. She thinks she can also hear his heart beating. Or is it hers?

The boy is looking at her and smiling.

'You're so beautiful,' he says. She is embarrassed and turns away towards their planet. She looks at the world which created her and wishes she could change the subject by saying that she comes from a beautiful planet. It was beautiful, once.

No one on Earth can see them now. They are completely left to their own devices, and to each other. Being in a little spaceship is perhaps the most intimate way to spend time with someone you love, she thinks.

Up here in space, day and night last only a couple of hours. But they have seen twelve sunsets and twelve sunrises, and above the clouds the sky is always blue.

The Letter on the Screen

She'd had supper with her dad and said good-night. All he could talk about was how she must never wear the red ring skiing again. Imagine if she had dropped it in the snow!

He was shocked that she had worn it when she went to meet Jonas. It would have been so easy for her to lose it when she took off her mittens or opened her pocket to read a text. Hadn't they told her the ring was a bit too big? That was why they had waited until her sixteenth birthday.

Now Anna was sitting in front of her computer in the blue attic room. She had finished writing the letter to her great-granddaughter and had put it on her pressure group's blog. As she wrote she had remembered more and more about what Nova had found on the Internet, but she composed the majority of the letter from scratch. She read through what she had written once again:

Dear Nova,

I don't know what the world will be like when you read this, but *you* know. You know how damaging climate change has been, how decimated the natural world has become and perhaps precisely which plants and animals are now extinct.

I am finding it difficult to write to you. It's not easy to write to someone who will live on the earth several generations after me. And knowing the person I am writing to is my own great-grandchild doesn't make it any easier. But I'll try to be as honest as I can.

Here where I live, in the richest corner of the world, there is still only one thing that counts. We call it consumption. In many other societies people talk about basic necessities. When we use words like 'consumption' I suppose it is because we don't want to see that there is an upper limit. The cup is never full. A word which is hardly ever used now is *enough*. Instead we overuse another word, which is shorter: *more*.

You know better than I do what the consequences of this will be, but already the ice over Greenland and the Arctic has begun to retreat, and the hunt for more reserves of oil and gas is on. Politicians say we must search for the last drop of oil because the world needs more energy. The world needs more oil and gas to lift more people out of poverty, they say. But they're lying. They know they're not driven by the interests of the poor. They know better than anyone that the rich countries' consumption of yet more oil and gas will only make matters worse for the very poorest. It is the oil companies and the richest oil-producing nations who want more profit. *More, more.* There is no political will to leave the remaining reserves of oil and gas alone. And there is no popular will. We are a selfish generation. We are a brutish generation. There is little understanding of the idea that the generations after us may need some of this energy. A word we rarely use is 'save'. But words like 'eco-conscious' and 'carbon-neutral' appear more and more in newspapers. We have developed a language, almost a nonsense-language, which has nothing to do with reality.

Is there really no cause for hope? Maybe, maybe not. All I can do is ask the question. You know the answer.

I don't have much of a solution to offer you. This is the best I can come up with. Try to imagine this scene:

Wherever people go – in mountains and forests, in market squares and on street corners, at underground stations and airports – green machines have been installed. You swipe your bank card and see the most wonderful images of nature, from all over the world. Some people will want to study a particular plant or animal; some a particular eco-system or habitat. The point is, you can only experience the parts of nature you are willing to contribute towards. All the money these machines make – millions of them could be installed all over the globe – is used to save our planet. And then there are competitions and lotteries to make the environment fun.

Perhaps a new type of slot machine is the world's best hope – although it hurts me to admit it.

But we will get nowhere by denying the truth of human nature or democracy.

There is so much that I don't know about the future. I only know that I have to be part of creating it. And perhaps I have made a small start.

With all the best wishes for you and the world where you will grow up.

Love,

Your great-grandmother Anna (Nyrud)

The clock struck twelve and it was her birthday. Now it was 12.12.12. She was almost surprised that nothing dramatic had happened as the minute-hand edged past midnight: there had been no collision at the petrol station, no avalanche of snow from the roof, no book falling from her shelves.

But shortly afterwards she received a text from Benjamin:

All good here. E liberated by Kenyan soldiers a few minutes ago. She's in good shape, just rang. Thanks for the moral support! Best, Benjamin. P.S. She was treated well, allowed to sit outside, wasn't tied up. Played dice with the hostage-takers! I went for the jog. B.

Anna breathed a sigh of relief and felt a tear form in the corner of her eye. She dialled Benjamin's number and he picked up:

'Is that you, Anna?'

'I was sure Ester would be set free on 12 December.'

'Why?'

'The world's gone in a loop, and we've crossed the threshold to a new era.'

'But *why*?'

'I don't think you've got the patience to listen to me explaining why. But this is my sixteenth birthday.'

'Happy birthday!'

'Thank you.'

'It's nice of you to ring, Anna, but after this you may have to wait a while before you contact me again.'

'I'll just tell you something then – in fact there's something I'd like to ask you.'

'Fire away! But let's keep this brief.'

'I still dream I'm my own great-grandchild . . .

And now I've seen her in the flesh. Are you sure I'm not ill?'

'You're not ill, Anna. Besides . . .'

'Yes?'

'Perhaps you're healthier than most. Perhaps more people should be like you.'

'How come?'

'We have to get better at visualising our heirs, better at recognising those who will inherit the world.'

'Nicely put!'

'Was there anything else you wanted to ask me?'

'Yes . . . Why do you have a star in your ear?'

He laughed:

'My wife gave it to me more than thirty years ago, a few days after Ester was born.'

'Cool!'

'Ester means "star". And not just any star. The morning star – or Venus.'

'I feel like an idiot!'

'Why's that?'

'Because I didn't guess.'

'Goodnight, Anna.'

'Goodnight, Benjamin.'

'Hang on a moment!'

'Yes?'

'Would you mind if I breached patient confidentiality?'

'Why would I mind? I've got nothing to hide.'

'Good. I'd like to send your regards to Ester. You remind me of her when she was your age. You have the same curiosity, the same determination.'

'I like that. Please say hello to her!'

'Strictly speaking, I'm not allowed to talk about my patients.'

'But I've said you can. It would very nice if you said hello and you can tell her about all the things we've discussed. By the way, you didn't prescribe me any treatment. You just confirmed that I didn't need any, so I wouldn't say that I've been your "patient".'

'You could be right there.'

'You're a friend, Benjamin.'

He laughed.

'Goodnight, Anna.'

'Goodnight!'

Anna got into bed. It felt like an eternity since she had last been there.

Perhaps it was because she was back in the bed

where she had woken up that she immediately remembered an important scene from her dream the
night before.

A Flaw in the Logic

It is early in the morning and the rain is pelting down. She is sitting in bed, in the blood-red room, and looking at her terminal screen. She thinks she is alone then realises that Nana is standing in front of the narrow window looking out across the valley. She coughs to let Nana know that she is not alone in the room. The old woman turns to her and says gently:

'Yes, my child?'

She reads aloud the letter she has just found: *I don't know what the world will be like when you read this, but* you *know . . .*

Nana steps back. She waves her left arm in the air and the red ring sparkles. It is as though she does it to show her power. She says:

'You've finally found what I wrote to you.'

'But how did it go with the green machines? Were they ever installed?'

Nana studies her and answers pointedly:

'Pass! I have to pass, Nova. Because whatever I say, there's a flaw in the logic.'

'Is there a flaw in the logic if I ask you what my great-grandfather was called?'

The old woman tosses her head, almost in a coquettish way.

'Don't you remember?' she asks. 'It's not so long since you were sitting on his lap. But the boy you're thinking of now is Jonas and came from Lo.'

'Jonas . . .'

'Haven't I told you how we used to ski to the old farm to meet up? In those days we just said "the mountains". Meet you in "the mountains".'

'That's right, yes. And now everything's overgrown.'

But great-grandmother Anna glares at her sternly and puts her in her place:

'Pass! There's another flaw in the logic now the world's been given a second chance.'

She swings her arm again and the polished ruby twinkles.

Great-Grandfather

Anna lay in bed listening to the creaking and crackling of the frozen walls. Just as she fell asleep she started to dream about a red bird pecking at the windowpane trying to get in. The dream was so realistic, and the pecking so intense, that she woke up. She switched on the light above her bed, grabbed her new phone and saw a text message. Perhaps that was what had woken her. Or was it the frost in the walls?

The text was from Jonas:

Are you awake?

She typed: *Yes. You woke me up.*

Happy Birthday!

Thanks, Jonas.

I've read it.

Read it? Read what?

What you wrote. You put it on the blog.

Wow! I didn't really think anyone would read it until seventy years from now. Can you ring me?

A second later, her mobile rang.

'You know it all turned out OK in Africa, don't you?' he said.

'Yes, I do, thanks. I spoke to Benjamin. Of course he's happy . . . Do you know why he has a star in his ear?'

'I'll never fear darkest night, for stars will show me the light . . .'

'No jokes now, Jonas.'

'Tell me then!'

'He was given the star by his wife a few days after Ester was born. And Ester means "star".'

Anna paused, and Jonas took the opportunity to wish her all the best for her birthday and say nice things about the letter she had put online. He was especially happy that she had written about his green machines. Then he coughed.

'I was struck by something you wrote at the end: "There is so much that I don't know about the future. I only know that I have to be part of creating it. And perhaps I have made a small start . . ."'

'Yes, I wrote that to my great-grandchild.'

He coughed again.

'I could offer my services as great-grandfather to that child.'

She laughed. She laughed so loudly that she was suddenly afraid she had woken her father on the floor below. She whispered into the phone:

'Come on then, Jonas!'

Then he burst out laughing.

'You're crazy,' he said.

'Lots of things are crazy.'

'Perhaps we can start by growing up together. I don't think we're in any rush to become a great-grandmother and great-grandfather.'

She laughed again:

'I want to do a lot more than just bring children into the world. In the summer I'm going to cycle to Bergen. Are you up for that?'

'If you take the train with me to Rome.'

'Do you promise?'

'Cross my heart!'

'Me too. Now we're talking. Can you get there via Holland?'

'Of course. The Dutch go to Rome. Would you like to see Amsterdam?'

'I would, but at the moment it's The Hague I have in mind.'

'The Hague? Do you have a hot date with a war criminal?'

'No, but one day an International Climate Court might be set up in The Hague. I fancy spending a day there with you. There's something I want to find out. Maybe there's something I'd like to show you: a big plot of land, a park perhaps . . .'

'I'm intrigued.'

'Jonas, do you promise me that we'll give this planet a second chance? And that we'll get lots of people to join us?'

'I do.'

'Do you really believe in this, Jonas? I want you to believe in what we're doing.'

'Yes . . .'

'Are you an optimist? Or are you a pessimist?'

'I don't know. Perhaps a bit of both. What about you?'

'I'm an optimist, Jonas. And do you know why? I think it's immoral to be a pessimist.'

'Immoral?'

'Pessimism is just another word for laziness. Of

course I worry. But that's different. A pessimist has given up.'

'You've got a point there.'

'We can't give up hope. And in practice that might mean we've got to fight. Do you want to be part of that, Jonas? Do you want to start a fight?'

'I think you could persuade me to do anything.'

'I'm going to hold you to that.'

'Go on then!'

'Shall we start reading together?'

'Reading?'

'Let's read Hamsun and Dostoevsky and the classics and Shakespeare and Homer. And old stories, *One Thousand and One Arabian Nights* . . . and mythology. We can start with the Greeks and the Norsemen. I want to read about Yggdrasil and Ragnarok. I want to read about Cassandra. She was a prophet who could predict the future, but no one believed her . . .'

'You mean reading aloud to each other? Isn't that . . .?'

'No, no, no. We read books at the same time. We lose ourselves in new worlds together. We create a large circle of imaginary friends. Then we can go walking in the mountains and take our gang with us.'

'OK. It's a deal.'

'Let's start tomorrow. I'll buy two copies of Hamsun's *Mysteries*. I saw it in the bookshop and fell for the title. It's my birthday, so I'm bound to get some money from Dad. Have you read it?'

'No. You never cease to amaze me.'

'That's good.'

'Maybe . . .'

'I think this is a crazy time to be alive, I mean, in a world on the edge of reason. It's actually quite different being sixteen years old from being fifteen and 364 days old. There's so much I want to do. Do you know what I'm going to do before I go to school tomorrow?'

'No. I'm not the psychic one.'

'I'm going to find out how many types of greenfly there are.'

'You *are* crazy.'

'But it was you who gave me the idea.'

'What? Me?'

'You wrote about it in your talk. You wrote that you wanted to set up foundations for all the threatened species of greenfly. So I've been wondering how many that would be.'

'I'd completely forgotten that. But now we should try to get some sleep.'

'Don't be so boring, Jonas. When you sent me the text I'd been asleep for a whole second, and now I feel wide awake.'

'I'm sure you'll fall asleep in no time after the day we've had. But won't your dad wake you at the crack of dawn? He'll be up in your room with currant buns and lemonade?'

'Sandwiches and tea, Jonas. I've grown out of buns and pop.'

'I'll say goodnight then!'

'Do you know what I'm going to do if I can't sleep?'

'Count sheep?'

'No, but you're almost right. I'm going to count greenfly. I'm going to close my eyes and count those bright, buzzing greenfly. And then I can tell you tomorrow how many I counted before I fell asleep.'

'I might do the same. Then we can see who fell asleep first. Goodnight, Anna. See you tomorrow!'

'Goodnight.'

The Village

It is night and pitch-black, but very hot. She is sitting on the ground on the outskirts of a village with three men her own age. In the bluish light of a gas lamp she sees that they are armed with automatic weapons. The gas lamp is hanging from the roof of a derelict shed. Two sacks of maize are propped against the walls. The sacks say *World Food Programme*.

From the bush around them she hears the chirruping of crickets. From the nearby village she hears some women chatting and laughing, a goat bleating, and now a baby crying. The crying stops abruptly and she imagines the child at its mother's breast.

She isn't frightened. But she knows where she is and who she is: that she is Ester and that she is a hostage in the borderland.

Bats flutter around the gas lamp. She looks at the hostage-takers. They nod, and she picks up some dice then throws them back on the red-brown earth. The dice roll between them, and all end up showing a six. She smiles with embarrassment. The men with the automatic weapons grimace.

'You win!' one of the captors shouts.

'White people always win,' says another, with an edge to his voice.

A bottle of red lemonade and four glasses are on the ground between them. One of the men pours.

She looks up. There is no moon, but in the sky there is the most magnificent cascade of stars she has ever seen. She cannot grasp how there can be so much war and hostility beneath this beautiful sky. She feels ashamed of mankind.

The intense chirruping of the crickets and the scattered sounds from the village just emphasise the peace of the night. There is something comforting about these familiar sounds in the darkness. They give her confidence.

But suddenly there is movement in the bushes, and the idyll is broken by the sound of shots and angry orders in a language she doesn't understand. One of the hostage-takers manages to fire his gun, but a minute later they are all lying on the ground begging for mercy. Ester, she does the same – she lies down and begs for mercy. The village women are now screaming in terror, and the baby starts to cry.

The hostage-takers are handcuffed and led to a green jeep that has appeared from nowhere. Ester is taken care of by an officer in a green uniform, who shouts in fluent English:

'Your father Benjamin sends his love!'

Ester

A nna had slept for a few brief hours, but when she woke up it felt as if she had been asleep for many months. She had been somewhere else, somewhere many miles away. Before the telephone rang, or perhaps at the same time, she remembered that she had been Ester and she had been taken hostage in the Horn of Africa.

She was expecting to hear Jonas's voice but instead she heard a woman's.

'Is that Anna?'

'Yes?'

'This is Ester Antonsen. I'm ringing from Nairobi.'

Anna was startled.

'I don't understand. Just this second I woke up

from a dream, and in the dream . . . I was you. Why are you calling?'

'To wish you a happy birthday! I hear you're sixteen today.'

'Thank you.'

'Dad told me. He was the one who suggested I ring you. You cheered him up when I went missing – I owe you!'

Anna was glad that she had helped Benjamin. She said:

'I told him it was fine to talk to you about me and to say hello. I really admire people like you who go out into the world and help the poor.'

Before she could add anything else, Ester asked:

'Is it true that you dreamed you were me?'

'Absolutely. I often dream I'm someone else. Once I dreamed I was an elephant. It was an odd feeling . . . being an elephant. But last night I dreamed I was you. How were you treated?'

'Basically, fine. I begged them to let me sleep under the stars. That was fine by them, and they took turns to watch over me. But we spent most of the night playing dice.'

'And you won!'

'How do you know?'

'Well . . .'

'Anna, how do you know?'

'How are the hostage-takers? They have wives and children . . .'

'They were handed over to the Somali authorities. Yes, I was treated with respect. But it wasn't an adventure, Anna. I was afraid. We cannot have aid workers being taken hostage. We can try to understand the terrorists, but we should never excuse terrorism. These boys may have to go to prison for a few years before they return home.'

'You're right . . . I'll re-think the "wives and children" bit.'

'What do you mean?'

'I saw a picture of you in the newspaper. Then I rang Benjamin. I suppose I recognised you from the photo on his desk.'

'But that's a photo of my mother. It was taken ages ago.'

'I know. So you must really look like . . .'

There was a silence at the other end. Then Ester said:

'I'm often told I'm a carbon copy of Mum. But she died when I was small, Anna. Since then my father has had only me. And then, after a while,

Lukas, my son. When I was captured, my father was frightened he'd lose me too, and perhaps even more frightened that Lukas would grow up without a mother.'

'I can understand that. He was very worried . . . How old is Lukas?'

'Eight. He loves his grandad – and it's mutual!'

'I can just imagine them together! I think of your father as a friend. Can you guess why?'

'Tell me.'

'Well, first of all he *understands* the climate problem, and he's engaged. But also he takes my opinions seriously even though I'm just sixteen.'

'But when *I* was sixteen I talked to Dad about exactly the same things. And he wasn't as open to them then. I've taught him.'

'Really? So you're your dad's teacher?'

'No, no. He taught me how to skim stones over water. He taught me about birds and how to make willow flutes and bark boats and wreaths.'

'He's been a good father then.'

'But it was me who joined Nature and Youth and came home and taught Dad about climate change. And I tell him about all the latest developments.'

'What are the latest developments?'

'Well, the glaciers are melting, and summer ice in the Arctic is the lowest it's ever been. This September was the hottest on record, and more than a thousand new weather records have been set in the US alone. We're seeing the side-effects of global warming even earlier than we expected to – it's worse than the most negative forecasts.'

'I know . . .'

'But the world can't agree on reducing CO_2 emissions. Oil-producing nations can't bear to leave their oil alone. The rich are unwilling to renounce their privileges. And the longer we wait for them to mend their ways, the more the damage is going to cost us.'

'Natural disasters must be costing us so much already.'

'They are. A few years ago, people said that we were the first generation to affect the climate on Earth and the last not to have to pay the price. That no longer applies. I have seen the effects with my own eyes, I have seen the drought, and I have held dying children in my arms . . . It hurts me so much, Anna, because we are not being killed by nature, we are being killed by ourselves.'

'When I've finished my education I'd like to work in the field just like you.'

'One day you can join me. But I'd love to meet you long before then.'

'I'm not sure I'll be as much fun as Benjamin has made out. I don't bite, though.'

'I'll be back in Norway next week. Do you ever come to Oslo?'

'Sometimes. But . . .'

'Yes?'

'I've got a boyfriend called Jonas . . .'

'I know.'

'I'm not sure I like the fact he told you.'

'Who?'

'Benjamin. He should have kept his oath.'

'It's no big deal, Anna. What were you going to say?'

'We've started a group at school – Benjamin suggested it. If you came to talk about your experiences in Africa, half the school would turn up. I'm sure we could use the school hall – and if we can't, we'll occupy it. You can tell us about the victims of global warming – and bring photos, if you have any.'

'I'd love to, Anna.'

'You can stay with us. You won't believe how

good a cook my dad is. Mum's not quite so good, but she's great at desserts.'

'That sounds really nice!'

'We've got a little guest room with a big sofa and seventeen different cushions . . .'

'Seventeen cushions?'

'. . . and each of the cushions is embroidered with a scene from a fairy tale. One shows Aladdin in the underground cave where he finds the magic lamp. Not many people remember that Aladdin also had a magic ring, but that's important to my story. I'll tell you everything when we meet. Have you ever ridden a camel, by the way?'

'Many times, Anna.'

'I've only done it once. Benjamin recommended I spend some time with Arabs – and I have.'

'Where?'

'Here, in my head . . . But now I can hear Dad in the kitchen. He'll be coming up the stairs in a minute. He's bringing me sandwiches and tea and thinks he's going to wake me. I can tell you much more when we meet. I'm looking forward to that! Now I'll just have to pretend I'm asleep.'

'Yes, you've got to play along.'

'Or should I say that Ester Antonsen rang me to

wish me a happy birthday and woke me up? Is that OK, do you think?'

'Of course. I haven't sworn any oath.'

'Goodbye then. Have a great day!'

'You too, Anna! This is your day!'

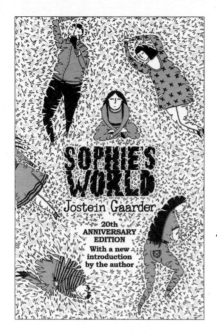

A beautifully designed 20th anniversary edition of *Sophie's World* with a new introduction by the author.

The perfect gift for anyone yet to discover this phenomenal novel, which has been translated into 60 languages and has sold over 40 million copies worldwide.

'A unique popular classic'
The Times

'It should be read by all'
Vogue

'A modern fairy tale'
Heat

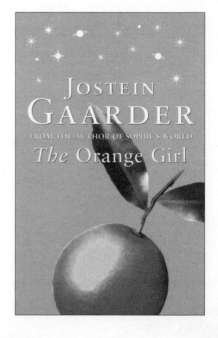

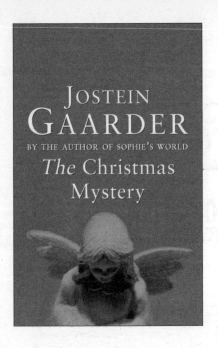

'A perfect Christmas tale'
The Times

'Anyone who enjoyed
Jostein Gaarder's
philosophical bestseller
Sophie's World will relish
The Christmas Mystery'
Sunday Times

'A masterful mixture of
fantasy and reality ...
a simply wonderful read'
She

'*The Ringmaster's Daughter*
confirms [Gaarder's] status
as one of Scandinavia's finest
literary exports and as a
novelist and storyteller of
outstanding calibre'
Herald

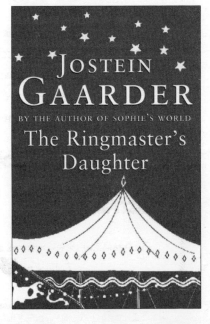

THE BOOKSELLER
INDUSTRY AWARDS
IMPRINT OF 2015
THE YEAR

For literary discussion, author insight,
book news, exclusive content,
recipes and giveaways, visit the
Weidenfeld & Nicolson blog and
sign up for the newsletter at:

www.wnblog.co.uk

For breaking news, reviews and exclusive competitions
Follow us 🐦 @wnbooks